"DO NOT FIGHT ME, QUERIDA . . .
Do not fight me," he murmured.

His mouth closed over hers. A wave gentled over them as they bobbed in the water. Her body began to explode with a frenzied passion she hadn't known she was capable of. In spite of her struggles, her flesh begged him to stay, to take, to conquer, to dominate.

"No," she breathed, but she knew in that moment that she could fight him no longer. Surrender was too sweet, too exquisite . . .

LAUREL CHANDLER, born in California, has also lived in such far-flung lands as Japan and Germany. She had planned a life as a professional ballet dancer, but finds writing much more exciting and rewarding. She is newly married and says of her husband, "Each day with him is a romance."

Dear Reader:

Well, this marks the sixth month that we have been publishing Rapture Romance, and the editors have only one thing to say—thank you! At a time when there are so many books to choose from, you have welcomed Rapture Romance, trying our authors, coming back again and again, and writing us of your enthusiasm. Frankly, we're thrilled!

In fact, the response has been so great that we now feel confident that you are ready for more stories which explore all the possibilities that exist when today's men and women fall in love. We are proud to announce that starting this month we will begin publishing four titles each month, because you've told us that two Rapture Romances simply aren't enough. Of course, we will not substitute quantity for quality! We will continue to select only the finest of sensual love stories, stories in which the passionate physical expression of love is the glorious culmination of the entire experience of falling in love.

And please keep writing to us! We love to hear from our readers, and we take your comments and opinions seriously. If you have a few minutes, we would appreciate your filling out the questionnaire at the back of this book, or feel free to write us at the address below. Some of our readers have asked how they can write to their favorite authors, and we applaud their thoughtfulness. Writers need to hear from their fans, and while we cannot give out addresses, we are more than happy to forward any mail.

Happy reading!

> Robin Grunder
> Rapture Romance
> New American Library
> 1633 Broadway
> New York, NY 10019

TREASURE OF LOVE

by
Laurel Chandler

RAPTURE ROMANCE
NEW AMERICAN LIBRARY
TIMES MIRROR

PUBLISHER'S NOTE

This novel is a work of fiction. Names, characters, places, and incidents are either the product of the author's imagination or are used fictitiously, and any resemblance to actual persons, living or dead, events, or locales is entirely coincidental.

Copyright © 1983 by Nancy L. Jones

SIGNET, SIGNET CLASSICS, MENTOR, PLUME, MERIDIAN and NAL BOOKS
are published by The New American Library, Inc.,
1633 Broadway, New York, New York 10019

First Printing, July, 1983

1 2 3 4 5 6 7 8 9

PRINTED IN THE UNITED STATES OF AMERICA

To Barbara, Dru, and Preshia
con muchas gracias

And to Wayne
con todo mi amor

Chapter One

❧

"So, Señorita Burton, I trust I have made myself clear?"

Jane glared at the man behind the map-strewn desk. Her blue eyes flashed with anger, but she managed to keep her voice steady as she replied.

"Oh, yes, Captain Pontalba. More than clear." Her small hands were clenched in her lap, sheltered from his view by the lace of her cuffs. Her dark blue suit was all wrong for the blazing heat of the Spanish summer, but she had hoped to make a good impression on the captain of *La Fortuna*. Apparently she had failed. He was still determined to treat her like a child.

The boat creaked, punctuating the silence that grew between them. Jane was hot and tired and near the end of her tether. She had been unflaggingly polite to this . . . *person*, but her patience was beginning to wear thin. She wasn't accustomed to having her credentials questioned, or her expertise brushed aside as unimpressive. Although she managed the largest diving school in San Diego, teaching hundreds of people each season to scuba, and although she still retained three university titles in competition swimming, this man refused to believe she could be of any use to him. It was galling, to say the least.

It also worried her. It had been a great sacrifice, leaving Uncle Chuck in charge for the summer. It was a terrible time for her to be gone: the school was in bad financial trouble, and her absence could only make it worse.

She understood her uncle's desire to keep his pact with his old friend Alejandro de Anza, but it was Alejandro's offer to share his portion of the treasure Francisco Pontalba sought that had brought her to Spain. Now, if only Alejandro could persuade Uncle Chuck to spend his days at the school, and not in the beachfront bars . . .

Right now, Francisco was leaning back in his chair, observing her. Behind him ranged a bank of equipment—radar, sonar, the magnetometer readout scope. Several composite photographs of the ocean bottom were tacked on the wall, the target areas circled in red. *"Aquí,"* someone had written in bold block letters. Here.

Quizás. Perhaps.

"I suppose that in your country I am a male chauvinist pig," he said pleasantly. "Your women's-libbers would cut me up in little pieces and feed me to the sharks."

"Yes, they would." And it would be such a waste, she found herself thinking, in spite of her consternation. He's so handsome. In fact, he's perfect.

Capitan Francisco Pontalba was tall, imposing, a conquistador in his impeccably cut European slacks, tailored shirt open to reveal a gold medallion around his long neck, and gleaming Italian loafers. His shirt sleeves were folded back, exposing bronze forearms and muscular wrists. A crown of raven hair curled just above his collar, and short sideburns accentuated the hollows of his cheeks. His nose was very straight, almost Arabic, and his lips were full and soft above a square jaw that looked as if it had been hewn from the trunk of a tree.

But it was his eyes that silenced the torrent of angry words that struggled to tumble from her lips. They were dark and flashing, like a thunderstorm on the Andalusian plains. A waste, indeed, to toss him to the sharks. But still, a very appealing idea.

"Don Francisco?" A bald man sporting a bushy beard and dressed in dungarees and a soiled T-shirt appeared at the door. He smelled of gasoline and motor oil, and his cheeks were smudged with grease.

"*Sí?*" Francisco gave his full attention to the man as they spoke in the rapid, sibilant Spanish of Castile, leaving Jane another chance to try to compose herself. She had a dozen good arguments to use to persuade him that she wouldn't be in his way, and she tried to prepare her defense. But the only thing that occupied her mind at the moment was his profile. It was aristocratic, so angular—the kind of silhouette one might see on an old coin. A doubloon, perhaps, or a piece of eight. . . .

"*Gracias, jefe,*" said the bushy-bearded man, bobbing his head and disappearing. Francisco caught the questioning look on Jane's face and smiled.

" *'Jefe'* means 'boss.' That was Carlos. He's my mechanic."

Carlos hadn't even glanced in Jane's direction. Perhaps he was used to seeing women in the navigation room. From what Alejandro had said, this "Jefe" Pontalba featured himself quite the ladies' man.

"Now, where were we, *señorita*?"

"We were discussing my role in this expedition," Jane said stiffly. "I suppose I should remind you that your partner himself asked me to accompany you."

"Ah, Alejandro." Francisco sighed, as if he were speaking to the man himself. "I don't blame him one bit for sending a third party to keep an eye on me. *Hostia,* what we're going after would test the honesty of a priest! But that doesn't mean that I have to humor you." His eyes bored through her and she squared her shoulders in defiance, yet inside, she felt herself go weak. Jet lag, she insisted. After all, she was on California time.

"I have heard how you teach scuba in San Diego," he went on. "And about your swimming contests. That's all very nice. But this is not a pleasure cruise. We aren't here to have fun. Millions of pesetas are at stake."

"But I'm fully able—"

"*Por favor,*" he said tiredly. "You don't understand. There is a great deal of difference between a gaggle of rich Americans who need to fill their idle hours with a hobby, and me and my men. This is our life. We can't play nursemaid to you just because Alejandro . . ."

He stopped speaking and stared at her, cocking his head. A faint smile crossed his full, soft lips. Jane shifted in her chair. Still he stared, his eyes taking in every detail of her appearance, from the loose cascade of honey-brown curls that tumbled to her shoulders, to her delicate features, to her slight figure. I know I look as helpless as a Victorian maiden, she wanted to tell him, but I'm far from helpless. I'm capable. I'm strong. I can swim as hard as any man on your vessel.

But she knew his mind was made up. She knew because she harbored the same stubborn streak, and she recognized it when she saw it. The spine stiffened, the hackles rose . . . Yes, this audacious Spaniard had already decided she was to be nothing more on his treasure hunt than unwanted ballast!

"Why are you staring at me?" she asked irritably, flushing as she realized that she herself had been staring at him for quite some time. Arrogant, yes. Condescending, yes. Infuriating, oh, yes.

Sexy, intriguing, arresting.

Yes, yes, yes.

"You look like someone very dear to me," he murmured, the harshness totally vanished from his tone. His husky, deep voice caressed her short temper, catching her off guard. It was as if he had physically touched her.

Who was he, that he could make her emotions yo-yo like this? After all, he was little better than a modern-day pirate, plundering the ocean for its treasures! He even looked like a pirate. All that was missing was a tricorne and an eyepatch.

Yet if she imagined the classic Spaniard, he also appeared. He was the medieval *don*, the matador, the conqueror of the Americas, a man who towered above other men.

And above women? She tried to look away. His unrelenting gaze was playing havoc with her pulse rate. I'm drowning, she thought, on dry land, in this man's eyes. Her heart began to hammer like a piston in an engine.

"You say I look like someone?" she managed, her throat gone dry.

"*Sí.* You are the figurehead of the galleon we seek. The lady of *El corazón.* She was a mermaid with long brown hair that twined around her body. Her eyes were as blue as the Mediterranean—like yours." He leaned toward her, studying her, and Jane fought to keep from catching her breath. Suddenly she remembered what it was like to run short of air beneath the waves.

"She's gone forever now," Francisco mused. "She must be. It has been too long. The waters around Mallorca are too warm for a sixteenth-century vessel made of wood; it would have decomposed in a few decades. Besides, the worms—*toredos*— must have devoured the entire ship by now." He gazed at a point beyond the room's walls, his eyes darkening with an intensity that unnerved her.

"But I'll find her grave. I'll find her treasure."

And I need to help, she pleaded silently. Please, let me help.

"*Bueno.*" His tone changed; he straightened the pile of maps on his varnished desk and rose.

"I mean what I say when I tell you that I will not allow you to jeopardize my search. You must obey my orders while you are aboard the *Fortuna.* No diving unless I give you permission. If I tell you to go below, you must. And no arguing about it. Do you agree?"

She hesitated, hating the way he was humbling her. She, who always played the captain back home.

His eyes changed in the light as he moved in front of the porthole, from tempest-tossed black to a more sensual, hypnotic gray. As he stood over her, so near, she could smell a subtle musk fragrance that cloaked him in elegance. He raised his hand to slice the air between them, like a magician creating an illusion.

"Within reason, *naturalmente*. I am a reasonable man."

Of that she was not convinced, but she dipped her head in surrender and cleared her throat. "All right, I'll follow your orders," she said, "but I really wish you'd let me prove myself to you."

His lids grew heavy as he smiled at her, his white teeth flashing. "On the sea, on our small boat, there will be plenty of opportunity for that."

A thrill jittered up her spine as she saw the lean, intent look that flashed over his craggy face. It was the look of the hunter sizing up his quarry. Feigning a composure she didn't feel, she smiled at him tightly and got to her feet.

"Would you mind showing me around before I go back to my hotel?" she asked. "I'm very tired, and if we're going to cast off before dawn tomorrow, I should get some rest."

He appraised her. "As you wish. Follow me."

She felt a momentary pang of disappointment, followed by distinct relief. Her ego had been fishing for a dinner invitation; everything else about her was glad to luxuriate in her last free hours before she would come aboard to live with him and his seven crewmen day in, day out, on this small boat.

The *Fortuna* had begun her life as a yacht, the plaything of a famous matador. His career had ended in the infirmary and his widow sold the boat to Francisco, who turned her into a salvage vessel. She was eighty feet long—not much space for nine people and all the equipment they carried—but she was sturdy and easy to handle. The navigation room had been added, and the once-spacious cabins redesigned to accommodate more people. But the name had remained—the *Fortune*. And, with a little luck, it would lead to a fortune which was lying beneath the sweet blue waters of the Mediterranean.

Francisco held the door open for her, stepping back with a sweeping gesture like the ghost of the matador furling his cape at a charging bull. Jane swept past, not noticing that the threshold was raised. Her heel caught. She began to tumble forward, unable to right herself because of her tight skirt. A moment's despairing image flashed through her mind—Jane Burton, token woman, sprawled on the deck in front of Francisco Pontalba's entire crew!

Strong arms wrapped around her waist. Instinctively Jane grasped them. Francisco's hands were so big that the fingers nearly met at the small of her back. Her whole body tingled as she held those hands, so strong, so full of life. They were warm, the tips callused from rough work. His ring fingers grazed her hipbones as he held her, righting her, then slowly turning her around to face him. They were so close that her breasts almost brushed his chest.

His touch flooded her with sensation, numbing her muscles until her legs almost buckled. Every inch of her was tingling, singing, as his hands tightened around her. His lips parted; so did hers. Oh, my God, he's going to kiss me, she thought wildly. Her body tensed.

Behind them, someone coughed. Francisco's eyes smoldered, but he let go of her and dropped his hands to his sides.

It was Carlos again. This time, Francisco introduced Jane to him. The man glowered, making it clear that he wasn't pleased by her intrusion into their business. Nodding shortly, he turned and left, even less subtle about his annoyance than Francisco had been.

Unconsciously Jane put a hand to her hair, her heart still pounding. Don't be silly, she chided. Of course he wasn't going to kiss you! Good Lord, he doesn't even know you!

Oh, but he was, another part of her protested. He was, and you wanted him to. . . .

As they followed Carlos, Francisco made sure she crossed the threshold safely and then shut the door behind him.

"Are you all right?" he asked.

Wordlessly she nodded.

"Then let's begin your tour." Gesturing toward the stern, he led the way through the coils of rope and wooden crates.

She counted six other crewmen, although they seemed to be everywhere at once as Francisco guided her through the pandemonium. Ernesto and José Luis were rolling up a length of nylon cord. Bernardo was helping Carlos with the engine. Ramón was talking on the radio, nodding with curt disapproval as Francisco explained that this was the woman who was coming with them. Coming from below, Hans—"German mother," Francisco explained—could barely conceal his hostility, but it was obvious that none of the men dared to challenge the decision of their *jefe*. If Don Francisco said the woman was coming with them, well, it was their fate to sail with bad luck on board.

Ricardo was the cook, a tiny, wiry man whose hands were lined and veined like those of the black-clothed old women Jane had seen hovering in front of the Gothic churches of Valencia. He alone welcomed her, smiling.

"How d'you do," he said in English. "I have cousin. Florida."

Overjoyed to find at least one friendly face, Jane shook his hand warmly and replied, "I'm fine, thank you. And how do you do?"

Ricardo shuffled. "I do, *gracias*."

Francisco smiled at the old man with obvious fondness. "*Bueno*, old one," he said, clapping him on the back, and asked if Ricardo would mind showing Jane around the galley.

Ricardo was obviously delighted to oblige. He drew her into the tiny cubicle and pointed proudly to a six-burner stove, making motions as if he were frying something in a pan.

"Propane," Francisco explained. "The refrigerator, too."

Ricardo's ears perked up. "*Refrigerador*," he announced, and opened the stainless-steel door with a flourish. The refrigerator was a huge thing, crammed with vegetables and cheese and many small bottles labeled in Spanish. A companion freezer contained bundles wrapped in butcher paper.

"That's our meat," Francisco told her. "Chicken, veal,

pork. We catch a lot of what we need when we're under way.''

''*Dulces*,'' Ricardo whispered. His eyes twinkled. Reaching into the freezer, he rummaged beneath the white packages. Then, grinning, he withdrew his hand and presented Jane with a frozen Mars bar.

''You,'' he said.

She laughed, delighted. ''Well, thank you!'' For more than just this candy bar, she wanted to tell him. ''*Muchas gracias*.'' She spoke with a Mexican accent, and Ricardo chuckled.

''You, Spanish?'' he asked. Jane shrugged.

''Just a bit,'' she replied in his native tongue.

''I didn't know that,'' Francisco mused, eyeing her with something that looked suspiciously like respect. Jane decided not to reveal just how limited her vocabulary was. She had studied Spanish for two years in college, but they were the first two years. Moreover, she didn't get many Spanish-speaking clients at the diving school, and she had just about forgotten what little she had learned.

Ricardo showed her the rest of the galley: his gleaming pots and pans, his lovely set of sharp knives. He pointed with one at Francisco.

''*El jefe*.'' Jane looked at him, puzzled.

''I like to cook.'' Francisco seemed embarrassed, as if he'd been caught doing something that he oughtn't. Woman's work, Jane guessed, or the work of old men.

''He do,'' Ricardo assured her. ''He do, do, do.''

''We should finish the tour,'' Francisco cut in. ''*Gracias*, Ricardo.''

The man bowed like a Chinese philosopher. ''*De nada*, Don Francisco.''

''Come, Señorita Burton.'' Francisco laid a hand on her arm, and she jumped. To hide her consternation, she busied herself with unwrapping the frozen chocolate bar, reminding herself that starting tomorrow she would be in close quarters with eight men. There would be no way to go off by herself for a break from all the foreignness, the hostility, or Francisco. What's going on with me? she asked sternly. I'm not a wide-eyed schoolgirl. For heaven's sake, I'm twenty-five years old and I've been around a man before!

"Are you ill?" Francisco asked, taking the Mars bar from her and deftly unwrapping it before handing it back to her. "Not getting cold feet, are you?"

She looked up. "Of course not."

"No, of course not," he rejoined. "Come, let me show you your cabin."

They took their leave of Ricardo. Leading the way over curled ropes and between pieces of gleaming metal, Francisco came to a ladder and began to climb down it.

Jane hesitated, aware that he would be able to simply tilt back his head and see straight up her skirt.

"Are you coming?" he called up to her, and she knew she had no choice.

"Yes," she breathed, skipping down with expert ease, thankful that at least the journey was brief.

Francisco inclined his head. *"Olé."*

She ignored his teasing, smoothing her suit jacket and wishing her palms would stop perspiring. Francisco led her down the dim corridor.

"Watch your head," he cautioned as he ducked down, and Jane chuckled. She was so short that the low bulkhead posed no problem for her.

Opening a door at the end of the corridor, he apologized, "It's small. But at least you have some privacy."

She was startled by the softness in his tone. Maybe he did realize how hard it was to be alone in a foreign country, resented by the people she would have to live with. Of course, he couldn't know how anxious she was about leaving everything in Uncle Chuck's hands. But it was kind of him all the same.

The room was tiny, no more than a bunk and a locker.

There wasn't even a mirror on the wall, but a nice round porthole framed a stunning view of the sea and the sky.

"The head—bathroom—is down the way, just beneath the galley."

She grinned. "I suppose that makes for a lot of jokes about the food."

He grinned back. "*Si*. Poor Ricardo. He will be happy to have an ally at last."

He checked his watch, gold against the dusk of his skin. "I'll take you to your hotel now. You must be exhausted."

"It's been a long day," she agreed. The longest she'd ever experienced. "But I can take a cab."

His brow creased. "Don't be ridiculous! I'll drive you."

She held up her hand. "You give the orders on the *Fortuna, señor*. On land, I'm a free woman."

Francisco leaned against the jamb and stared at her, then shook his head. "You're not what I expected, Señorita Jane Burton. Not what I expected at all."

"Neither are you," she retorted.

Not by a long shot, she thought, remembering the scene as she stepped into the tepid bath the maid had drawn for her in her hotel room. Oh, she had known he would be difficult. Alejandro and Uncle Chuck had warned her. But she hadn't expected a throwback to the Middle Ages!

Uncle Chuck. If it weren't for him, she wouldn't be here today. She didn't know what on eatth would have become of her. She still didn't remember the car accident, nor the three days that followed, when her parents quietly passed away. She did remember sitting up in her hospital bed and seeing the stranger who was Daddy's brother, holding a stuffed pink kitten in his arms. When he saw that she was awake, he clutched it against his chest and burst into tears. "I'll take care of you, Janey," he sobbed. "As if you was my own."

Well, he had done his best, she thought as she drew a fragrant bar of Maja soap along her arms and collarbones.

But her uncle was a drifter, a dreamer, and even though he gave up the sea and tried to settle into fatherhood, his heart had never stopped wandering. Night after night, ten-year-old Jane sat in the wicker rocker by the window of their ancient Ocean Beach cottage in her cotton nightie, waiting for Chuck to return. He always did, laughing and singing, a strange, sweet odor on his breath. Then he'd tell her to look in his jacket pockets for her present—an aluminum pouch of cocktail peanuts, compliments of the bartender at the Surf's Up Bar and Grill.

He tried, he really tried. He made it to her sixth-grade Christmas pageant, though he didn't make it to her graduation, and he was drunk the first time she brought a date home. She loved him, but she learned very quickly not to depend on him.

But he did give me the sea, she thought as she splashed in the claw-footed tub. She could still remember the first swimming lesson, she clinging and screaming, he bobbing and laughing. But she was so eager to please him that soon she was streaking through the water like a little fish, entranced by the fairy kingdom beneath the surface. It was a magical world, with fans of coral and fish decorated more outrageously than the ones in her coloring books. The sea became her friend, the thing that always embraced her when Chuck forgot to. . . .

As the years passed, she spent more time in the water than out of it. She shone in competition; she was the local champ, beating all the boys with ease. Chuck was so proud of her that he hardly ever missed a meet.

Then there were the underwater diving lessons. She grew to love the world of water with a fierce devotion, reveling in the silence, the mystery. The kelp beds undulated around her, their long green strands beckoning like the fingers of an undersea lover. For many years the sea was her only lover, and she worshiped it with a passion that most women never experienced, not even for the men in their lives.

Men. Was she just bad at picking them? she wondered as she soaped her breasts and trickled water on them. They were all like Uncle Chuck—wandering, undependable. Nobody had matched her in drive or strength. Sooner or later they had all let her down: Jack, who had charmed her into doing his homework; Bill, the diving instructor she ultimately had to fire for goofing off. Sometimes she wondered if there were a single man in the world who could satisfy her.

But she had never had much time to brood about such things. At her urging, Chuck quit his job as a longshoreman and opened up a little diving school. She knew he wouldn't help out much, and he didn't disappoint her. While she put in long days, he swaggered around the beach, bragging about how Burton Diving had started out so small, and now it was the biggest in the whole damned county.

"The whole damned county!" she heard him crow as he burst into the office the fateful day that had led her to this hotel room in Valencia. He had a stranger in tow, a tall white-haired man who smiled happily at Uncle Chuck and clapped him on the back.

"Janey, this is ol' Alejandro de Anza, my *compadre*. He's the best friend I have in the whole world. What'd I tell you, Alex? The cutest thing this side of Madrid!"

Hiding her surprise, Jane shook hands with the man. Uncle Chuck was full of tall tales about his exploits with the fabled de Anza. He and Chuck had met while Chuck was stationed with the Navy in Rota, Spain. They had spent every free moment searching for sunken treasure or pirate booty buried in the sand beneath the ocean—searching, but never finding.

"I am enchanted," said Mr. de Anza. His accent was thick and foreign-movie-sexy.

Her uncle looked so raggedy beside his old friend, she thought sadly. The Spaniard was obviously ill; his hands shook and he coughed often. But he retained an air of self-assurance that was missing in his American friend. Chuck's face was always ruddy, as if he had a perpetual sunburn, but the veins on his nose were broken and his eyes were rheumy. He was already a balding old sailor, although he hadn't been to sea for fifteen years, since Jane had come into his life.

"Come on, let me show you the pool," Chuck said. "We'll be right back, Janey. Then you can show off your great cooking!"

She grimaced. Her great cooking currently resided in three Tupperware bowls. Tonight's menu featured leftovers of leftovers.

"Perhaps you would prefer to dine out," de Anza suggested. "My treat."

She smiled at him as he followed Chuck out the door. "I'd love it."

"*Bien*. Then we shall do it."

He gave her a brief nod and disappeared. Jane bent to her accounts-payable ledger with a lighter heart, managing not to panic as she added up the sums they owed their impatient creditors. She liked this friend of Uncle Chuck's, and the evening promised to be interesting.

Then her uncle bellowed so loudly that she jumped out of her chair: "*El Corazón?* You're *sure?*"

There was a lot of "shushing" followed by low, cautious mumbling. Then, "Christ, Alex, I can't go either. I'm too damned old," and finally she heard Alejandro say, "Jane? But she's just a girl! And Francisco would have a heart attack!"

Jane pulled the plug and stepped gingerly out of the tub. Well, he hadn't had a heart attack, but he was just as unhappy to see her as Alejandro had promised, and he was every inch the arrogant Latin both he and Chuck had warned her about.

"You Spaniards are terrible, eh, Alex?" Chuck had laughed, elbowing his friend. De Anza had nodded, frowning. Clearly he was concerned.

"You see, *señorita*, Francisco will be playing by a different set of rules than you. He's a Spaniard; Spanish women know what to expect from him. They know how to deal with him. But you . . ." He trailed off. "Please do not be insulted. I feel a certain responsibility toward you." He scratched his chin.

"Perhaps this is not a good idea, Chuck. I can find a male diver somewhere. Perhaps if I offer him a share, I will be able to trust him."

"Bilge!" Chuck cried. "When I left Spain, we promised we'd help each other if we ever needed it. You've got to have somebody on that boat you're sure of, if the treasure's as huge as you say."

"It is," Alejandro assured him. "Millions of pesetas' worth of gold coins, rubies, emeralds."

Jane was wild with excitement. Millions! This could be the break they needed! "Please, Mr. de Anza, let me go. I can handle anything."

"That's true, Alex. I've never met a man yet Janey couldn't handle."

Jane shook herself from her wool-gathering and gave her reflection a rueful smile in the bathroom mirror. She thought of Francisco's haunting eyes, the jolt of his skin against hers, the near-kiss in the navigation room.

"Well, Uncle Chuck," she said aloud, "I think ol' Janey's finally met that man."

Chapter Two

Jane tossed and turned in the luxurious hotel bed, dozing into dreams of pirates and galleons and Francisco, looming against a sky filled with smoke and flame. Clad in a billowing white shirt and hip boots, cutlass drawn, he was ready to board the hapless ship that had dared to cross his path on the high seas.

And she, a Victorian lady in a tea-colored lace gown with honey curls atop her head, was fighting against his broad chest as he swept her up in his arms, claiming his prize, the spoils of victory, of conquest. . . .

She sat up. It was three-thirty. The last time she had looked, it was three-twenty-five. It seemed that the luminous hands of her traveling alarm clock hadn't moved all night. Would the dawn never come?

He would be here at five-thirty. Squinting into the darkness, she saw her scuba gear and her small duffel bag lying by the door. A pair of jeans and a red-and-white-striped T-shirt lay over the satin chair in front of an ornate dressing table. Her heavy bedspread, pulled back the night before by the maid, was a concoction of silk and ruffles that would have made Marie Antoinette swoon with envy.

The modern American woman invades the boudoir of the Old World Spanish lady, Jane mused.

And the domain of the old-fashioned Spanish male, as well. She remembered when she was little, the only girl in their little beachfront community, and all the boys had started a secret club in the bait shop. Their first order of business had been to erect a sign that said "No Girls Allowed." She had stood outside and cried and cried, until Uncle Chuck had returned from the Surf's Up and comforted her with a new snorkel.

Now she was in the clubhouse, and the boys were furious, except Ricardo, who was sort of a minor player anyway, being "just the cook." Perhaps that was why he had been so kind to her, or maybe he simply enjoyed showing off his galley to a pretty foreigner who admired his skill and listened to his broken English.

"He do, do, do," she murmured aloud, closing her burning eyes. "Oh, Francisco Pontalba, why are you such a male chauvinist pig?"

She was dressed and finishing the last of her room-service rolls and thick, rich coffee when Francisco came for her. Dressed in a pair of blue corduroy trousers and a sweatshirt that said "Universidad de Salamanca," he seemed younger somehow, more boyish. There was something vulnerable yet undeniably sexy about the exposed length of tanned bare skin at the nape of his neck. His jet hair, still damp, curled into ringlets above his heavy lids. He smelled of soap and a subtle fragrance that was his alone. Blindfolded, she would have known that it was he who stood before her.

The medallion still hung around his neck, the chain hiding among the tufts of curly black hair that peeked above his sweatshirt. She thought of her dream, of his pirate garb slashed to the waist. I wasn't far off, she found herself thinking.

There was an air of eagerness about him that was palpable. To find *El Corazón* was his dream, Alejandro had told her. Francisco had yearned all his life to wrest her buried treasure from the jealous bosom of the sea.

Well, it was her dream to save her business. It was not as romantic, perhaps, but it was just as important to her.

"No tight skirts today," he said by way of greeting. His quick eyes took in her appearance, her jeans and ratty tennis shoes. Her hair fell freely over her shoulders, waves and curls that rippled through the strands of brown and blond. Did she really look like his mermaid? she wondered. Or was that just part of his "Latin-lover" routine?

"This is everything?" He seemed surprised as he hefted her small canvas bag over his shoulder and took up her air tanks.

"Yes. I travel light."

His eyes flickered. "*Bueno.* I was afraid you would be foolish enough to pack cosmetics and hair curlers." His eyes rested on her naked face, free of makeup, and she couldn't help the blush that rose to her cheeks. In Spain, the women were always perfectly coifed, their faces expertly adorned before they dared to venture outside. She must appear drab, compared to them, as well as haggard from lack of sleep.

He cleared his throat. "We must go. Everything is in order downstairs. Have you got your passport in a safe place?"

"Yes. It's with my traveler's checks. And I changed some money at the airport."

"You came well prepared." He opened the door and stepped into the hall.

No, I didn't, she almost replied. I certainly wasn't prepared for you.

Giving the room a final scan, she joined him in the hall and followed him toward their adventure.

Sea gulls circled the *Fortuna* as the crewmen made the preparations for casting off. Jane could hear their excited voices through her porthole as she stowed her gear. This is it! she thought. Soon we'll be on our way.

San Diego was half a world away. How would Chuck cope with the summer rush without her? Alejandro had been more than generous, paying for an extra assistant for the season and offering to keep watch over Chuck, especially when she knew the old man's heart was with the *Fortuna* this morning. It must have cost him dearly not to see them off.

Sighing, she looked around. There was nothing left to do but go topside, although after her reception the day before, she wasn't eager to face the crew again.

Still, she couldn't hide out for the whole trip. Sooner or later she was going to have to get acquainted with these men, and she knew from experience that stalling would only make her task more difficult.

She took one last glance around, tucking her T-shirt into her jeans; then she opened the door and climbed the ladder to the upper deck. The first one to see her was Carlos, the bald man. He nodded brusquely and continued on his way toward the bow of the boat. Jane gave him a tentative smile, but he had already brushed past her.

Overhead, the gulls circled and squealed, swooping into the water in search of a tasty breakfast. The boat rocked with the slapping of the waves. Spice and salt permeated the air. It was a perfect day.

Around her, the crew worked, carrying things to and fro, calling to each other in bursts of monosyllables.

"Perdón," Ernesto muttered, nearly colliding into her with a big wooden crate. Jane swerved around him, only to crash into Hans, who snorted in disgust as his nylon rope unrolled around Jane's feet.

"I'm sorry," Jane said. She felt he was at fault, too, but apologizing seemed the prudent thing to do.

"Cisco! Cisco!" A high-pitched call caught Jane's attention.

A woman stood on the dock. She was beautifully dressed in a pastel sundress that wafted in the breeze like the gossamer wings of a butterfly. Her makeup was very heavy, almost a mask, and the smile that crossed her lips was a scarlet gash.

Francisco appeared from the stern and waved to her, eyes dancing. Then he saw Jane and Hans, still disentangling themselves. A cloud passed over his features and he jerked his head toward the ladder that led to her cabin.

"Go below decks," he ordered. "You're in the way of the

men.'' Then he turned away, and smiling at the lady, began to walk down the gangplank.

Jane's mouth fell open. In the way? Dammit, she hadn't had time to be in the way! Her run-ins with Carlos and Hans were unfortunate accidents. She knew how to comport herself on a boat.

She stood there seething as he reached the other woman and helped her onto the plank, all chivalry and charm. The pair laughed and chatted as they strolled back. Obviously the lady was coming aboard. And obviously Francisco didn't think *she* was going to be in the way!

Jane turned on her heel and stomped toward the ladder. Apparently his girlfriend hadn't seen her. But of course not; she had eyes only for her darling.

"*Hola*, American!'' Ricardo called out. The cook was carrying a string sack full of onions.

Buenos días,'' Jane returned, managing to quell her anger long enough for a few friendly words.

Pointing to the galley, he indicated that he wanted her to come along. She hesitated. Francisco had banished her to her cabin, but she would be just as out of the way in the galley. Unless, of course, he didn't want his girlfriend to know there was a woman on board.

"Come,'' Ricardo urged her in Spanish. He rubbed his stomach in a theatrical way that almost made Jane laugh despite her pique.

"All right, I will!'' She gave her hair a defiant toss and followed his lead.

As soon as they were inside the galley, Ricardo hung the onions from a hook in the ceiling and put on a white apron. Then he rubbed his hands together, as if in anticipation, and opened the refrigerator.

"*Fresas*,'' he announced, pulling out a huge dish of hulled strawberries. They were as big as a man's thumb, and so red that they positively glowed. It had been a long time since her rolls and coffee, she realized.

Ricardo raised his brows. *Sí?"*

"Sí," She answered, plucking one from the bowl and popping it in her mouth. He had dusted them with sugar, and they were delicious.

They sat in companionable silence, picking out the biggest berries for each other, giggling when Ricardo dropped one and it bounced inside his apron pocket. Some of Jane's tension began to slide away from her. What did it matter to her if Francisco had a girlfriend? Or maybe even a wife. He was nothing to her, merely a haughty man who was so prejudiced against women that he couldn't believe she would be of any help on the hunt. Naturally, he wouldn't want to parade his unwelcome American guest before his woman. Spanish ladies were reported to be very jealous—as were Spanish men. . . .

Francisco's lyrical Spanish wafted toward them on the silky breeze, answered by the staccato phrases of the woman.

"Who is that lady?" Jane asked as casually as she could.

Ricardo grinned. "Cousin."

"Oh." Jane bit into another strawberry. The sense of relief she felt was ridiculous. For God's sake, she barely knew the man!

Except that he was tall, and handsome, and carried himself with the bearing of a king.

"Well, how do you like your cabin, Miss Burton?" Francisco asked as he walked into the galley, unaccompanied.

Jane kept her face a mask. "I didn't think it mattered too much where I went," she said calmly, "as long as I stayed out of everyone's way."

"I was looking for you. I wanted to introduce you to Señorita Ybarra. Esperanza was very eager to meet you."

"I apologize. I would have liked to meet your cousin, too."

He looked puzzled. "She's not my cousin. "Who told you that she was?"

"Cousin," Ricardo said proudly. Jane flushed. Now Francisco would know that they had been discussing him!

Francisco said nothing for a moment. Finally he picked a strawberry out of the bowl and ate it, then, without looking up, spoke. "She's Alejandro's niece. And I believe I told you to go to your cabin, not the galley. I expect you to do as I say aboard my ship. I thought I had already made my feelings quite clear."

Jane lifted her chin. "Yes, you did. If you'll excuse me, I'll go there right now."

At her defiant tone, his head lifted suddenly, and his eyes burned into her. They stood silently, regarding one another.

"I'll escort you," he said.

"I know the way," she replied, moving past him. She had a feeling she would be able to find it in her sleep before the treasure hunt was finished.

"I said I'll take you," Francisco shot back. He wrapped his hand around her arm and led her out of the galley.

"Mr. Pontalba, let go of me! You might be the captain of this boat, but you're not the lord of the manor. This is the twentieth century, you know."

"*Señorita*, I have a lot to attend to. I don't have time to argue with you." He pointed to the ladder.

Although she glared at him, he stood his ground. Obedience once again seemed her only choice, but with each step she took down the ladder, it galled her.

"Thank you," Francisco said as he joined her in the corridor. They walked toward her room.

"Did you know that my cabin is across from yours?" he asked conversationally as he opened her door and escorted her inside.

How convenient. He could stand guard over her all night, she thought hotly.

"As soon as we have maneuvered out of the dock, I will call you topside," he promised .

"You're too kind." She sat on the edge of her cot and

folded her arms, wishing she had thought to bring the new books she had bought on marketing and sales. It looked like she might have a lot of time on her hands for reading.

She didn't look up as, leaving, he closed the door. This was so humiliating! She'd taken dozens of ships just as large as this out for scuba parties. Of course, they didn't carry the sophisticated gear that the *Fortuna* did, but she was no stranger to radar and other navigational devices, and she was a top-notch sailor. The row of trophies from boat races standing on the mantel back home attested to that!

The boat lurched as the motors revved. Slowly it began to move. Jane watched from her porthole, wishing she could be on deck in the salty wind and the sunshine. Instead, thanks to Francisco, she was efficiently stashed away like a piece of cargo in the hold.

The pirates were boarding the ship. Jane flung herself in front of Richard, the wiry French cook, who was guarding the precious treasure they carried. Hearts of gold, hundreds of them, were stacked on the deck. Easy pickings for the thieves.

Scroungy buccaneers flung her aside and began to load the golden hearts into their pockets. Then, their master strode on deck, his boot heels clopping on the planks. He stopped and surveyed the scene, hands on hips, feet wide apart, until he saw Jane, lying where she had been pushed, trembling with fear. The smoke clouded his face, but his eyes burned through the gray curtain like two glowing coals.

"My prize," he announced. He scooped her up in his arms and crushed her lips to his. Violent tremors raged through her as she fought against the wild pleasure she felt, and then she weakened in his grasp, returning his kiss. . . .

"Señorita Burton, please wake up. You have been asleep all day."

Jane's eyes flew open. Francisco towered over her, his face

painted a brilliant sheen of red by the dying sunlight from her porthole.

"I . . ." she began, still drowsy. Her gaze traveled down the length of his body; he had changed his long pants and sweatshirt for jogging shorts and a sleeveless T-shirt that exposed the long, well-developed muscles of his arms and legs. Although she usually spent most of her waking hours around men dressed in swim trunks and little else, it made her uneasy to see so much of Francisco's body. He was too virile, too . . . sexual, she thought, searching for, and finding, the right word.

"We're having *la cena*," he went on, his voice gentle and coaxing. "Dinner. You must come and eat. Or your boy-friend will be wounded." His eyes twinkled. "Ricardo's prepared a special dinner in honor of you."

"Well, how nice," she said lamely as the memory of her dream seeped into her mind. Richard the French cook, the guardian of hearts. And Francisco the pirate, the robber of them.

She sat up, and he moved away. "I'll see you above," he said. "We have erected the sun awning. We'll be eating there."

"Thank you."

He bobbed his head in a courtly gesture and left her.

Charming. He was utterly charming when he wanted to be, she thought. Was this his way of apologizing?

She found her brush in the scarlet-tinted cabin and drew it through her hair as she thought about Francisco. He had a lot on his mind, certainly. If she were captain here, she might be edgy, too, having a foreigner around.

Setting down the brush, she gathered her hair in a ponytail and slipped a shell-encrusted clasp around it. She wasn't behaving very well, she had to admit. It had been thoughtful of him to wake her up, especially when he was so busy.

The red-and-white T-shirt was damp with perspiration. She

exchanged it for a cool cotton blouse with a scoop neck and capped sleeves, then headed eagerly for the deck.

As she emerged from the top of the ladder, she caught her breath. The sky was a riot of reds and pinks and purples, flung across the heavens as if from some giant's palette of paints. The few clouds that hovered in the air were tinged with vivid scarlet, wisps of flame in a fiery expanse of unbelievable beauty. Beneath them, the water was a startling azure, the purest blue Jane had ever seen. The ocean was as tranquil as a silent, snowy forest. Only the soft creaking of the ship and men's low voices, the clanking of cutlery, disturbed the utter silence.

Bewitched, she turned around and took in the view on the starboard side. A row of limed, whitewashed buildings nestled on the cliffs. The sun glanced off them, rose-golden, many-faceted jewels in the magical light. Pines grew right down to the beaches, their verdant bows dipping in the salt-white stretches that were cooled by riplets of ocean waves.

"Ibiza," Francisco murmured behind her. "Mallorca's next. And after that . . . we find my lady of the sea."

"It's so beautiful," Jane said.

"Very beautiful," Francisco echoed. The back of her neck tingled and she nodded without looking at him. A guitar began to play a mournful, sweet melody and her heart filled with it as she turned to face her pirate.

The sky was a magnificent backdrop for his haunting good looks. The dying sun brushed his high cheekbones with mauve shadows, warmed his dark eyes with flecks of bright gold. The breeze ruffled his wavy raven hair, trailing it away from his high forehead, accentuating the Moorish angles of his face. Jane felt awed by the very sight of him, by his perfection. He looked like a painting of a lord in chiaroscuro.

Then she realized how he was looking at her—intently, hungrily—and she shook herself out of her reverie. Don't forget that this is the man who sent you to your cabin like a little child, she reminded herself. This is the man who holds your fortunes in his hands.

Raising her chin, she gestured toward the galley. "I'm starved," she said in a too-loud voice, doing her best to break the mood.

Saying nothing, he continued to regard her, his eyes narrowing in an almost cruel way. He was appraising, calculating. It wasn't the kind of look she was used to—not the shy glances of her students nor the falsely arrogant leers of the deep-sea fishermen and boat owners. It was almost primitive—no, it *was* primitive, and it shook her. It was new; he was new, and she didn't know how to deal with him.

"Why are you always staring at me?" she said suddenly, struggling to hide her confusion. Though his lips moved in reply, he didn't take his eyes off her.

"I always stare at beautiful things," he answered, his voice gravelly and hushed.

She started past him, retorting, "I'm not a thing," but he took possession of her hand. Electricity crackled through her, and her heart began to pound.

"Let me escort you to the *cena*." Without waiting for her permission, he led her to the stern of the boat, where Ricardo and the others already lounged around a makeshift table. Some of the men were sitting on the deck; others had pulled up boxes. Carlos, who was playing the guitar, nodded his head at her; the others regarded her curiously. Their eyes moved from her to Francisco and back again in speculation. She flushed under their scrutiny, wishing they would accept the fact that she was here to stay and let down their guard. But their silence, their eyes, told her that they weren't about to take a woman into their precious male circle.

Ricardo grinned at her, proudly pointing to the huge wooden bowl in the center of the deck. "Paella," he said. "I give." He began to fill a plate with the mixture of rice, saffron, and seafood.

With a weak smile, Jane raised her hands. "Too much!" she cried.

Ricardo shrugged and added two more spoonfuls. Then he handed her the bowl.

Francisco turned and spoke sharply to Ernesto, who was seated in one of the two deck chairs. Mumbling, the man rose from the chair and found a place on the deck. Francisco pointed to the newly vacated seat.

"If you please, *señorita*," he said. His tone was formal, distant, as if he had not devoured her with his eyes only moments ago.

"Oh, no," she said, moving away. "Ernesto was there first. He can have . . ." She trailed off as she watched his lips purse together in a sour frown of disapproval.

"My men," he said tightly, "are gentlemen. In Spain, we know how to treat our women."

She arched one delicate blond brow. "Do you?"

He said nothing, only stared at her, waiting. Sensing the growing interest of the crew, she sat in the chair with as much dignity as she could muster and settled her plate in her lap.

"*Bien*," Francisco said. He reached for another deck chair—which obviously had been reserved for him—and pulled it near hers. "There's a play," he went on. "*The Taming of the Shrew*. You would do well to read it, I think."

Jane's mouth dropped open. "Why, you . . ." she began, but her anger silenced her. How dare he! Just who did he think he was?

Ricardo gestured impatiently. "You do!" he ordered, making motions to indicate that she should take a taste.

That was one order she had no trouble obeying. She hadn't eaten anything since the strawberries.

Ignoring Francisco, she lifted her fork to her lips. The paella was delicious, filled with the flavors of the sea and of Spain: saffron and shrimp, small clams and mild fish, dark black olives and tender peas. It was nothing like the paella she had tried back home in San Diego, with its frozen bay shrimp and packaged rice. Her eyes widened in appreciation.

"*Gracias*," she told the eager cook. "*Deliciosa!*"

Ricardo chuckled. He pointed to the various bits and pieces in the dish. "*Langostino*," he told her.

Francisco turned to her. "Lobster," he explained.

Ricardo rattled off some more ingredients.

"Shrimp," Francisco continued. "Clams. Baby eel."

She almost gagged. Her stomach lurched. With great deliberation she swallowed the bite in her mouth. "Eel?" she asked weakly, darting a glance at the heap of food on her plate.

"Is something wrong, *señorita*?" Francisco asked, but she could tell he understood her agitation.

Ricardo looked worried, murmuring something to his chief.

"Ricardo wants to know if something has displeased you." Francisco's lips twitched, and she wanted to smack his sassy face for the delight he was taking in her discomfort.

"No. Nothing at all," she replied coolly, jamming her fork into the paella and taking a hefty bite. "I love it. It's the best thing I've eaten in months."

Ricardo relaxed and dug in, obviously savoring the results of his skill.

"My compliments," Francisco said, slinging a leg over the side of his chair. "At least you have manners."

She stared at him, speechless, as Francisco turned his attention to his plate and to his crew. The men chatted, patently ignoring her.

She turned to Ricardo. "In the United States," she told him in shy, halting Spanish, "I swim. I teach to swim. Scuba." Ricardo raised his brows.

"*Sí?*" He questioned her rapidly, too quickly for Jane. She cocked her head, straining to understand.

"He wants to know if you'll be diving with us," Francisco said, scraping the meat from a small, delicate clam and closing his soft lips around it.

She eyed him. "What should I tell him?"

"It's not likely," he replied without hesitation.

Jane frowned. "I'm perfectly capable—"

"I don't care. I signed on seven men. I only needed seven. *Men.*"

Jane shook her head. "You're impossible," she snapped. "I could help out a lot. I really could. But you're so macho—"

Watch it, calm down, a voice inside her whispered. Summoning all her effort, she clamped her mouth shut and toyed with her fork. *The Taming of the Shrew*, indeed!

A few of the men chuckled, and she realized that they had understood the word "macho." And approved of it, no doubt. They probably cheered every time Francisco pushed her around.

Ricardo held out the bowl of paella, offering more. Her plate was still full, and she realized that he was trying to smooth over the situation for her.

"*Gracias, no.*"

"Lost your appetite?" Francisco asked. "Too many strawberries? Or too much of my macho company?"

"No, I'm fine. I don't eat much." She was lying shamelessly. She was famous on the bay for the amount of food she wolfed down. "Bottomless Burton," they called her, although the second meaning of the ribald nickname didn't hold true. She could wear a bikini with the best of them.

"I apologize," she said reluctantly. "This is your boat. Your hunt. I told you I wouldn't argue."

He scratched his chin. "A big concession, coming from such a stubborn *niña*. I have the feeling it will be the first of many."

Jane took another bite of paella. Silently, and reluctantly, she agreed with his prediction.

The sky had darkened; faint washes of gray muted the spectacular colors. There was a whoosh of wings above them as the seabirds returned to land for the evening.

"I'm going into the water tomorrow morning," Francisco said. "Would you care to accompany me?"

"Yes." She seized on his offer as the chance she needed to prove herself to him. "Are we diving?"

He seemed pleased by her eager response, his eyes flaring slightly as he lounged in the chair. Catlike, Jane thought, like a leopard waiting to pounce.

"No. Just swimming." He set down his plate and rose. "*Gracias, Ricardo. Buenas noches, hombres.*"

Then, without another word, he walked into the dark. Jane stared after him, startled by his abrupt departure.

"He do," Ricardo explained helpfully. Jane cocked her head.

Ricardo made motions as if he were looking at a map. Immediately she understood: Francisco was off to continue his love affair with his lady of the sea.

She awakened to find that the water had cast shimmering ripples of blue against the bulkheads of her cabin. It was like floating inside a grotto of brilliant cerulean. Peering out her porthole, she caught her breath at the splendor of the early-morning sun on the Mediterranean. Vibrant blue and dazzling gold were combined like fine cloisonné on a mermaid's hand mirror.

In the distance, a trio of dolphins breached the surface, arcing like arrows as they frolicked in the still water. She followed their antics with a bemused smile on her face, until another, closer figure caught her attention.

It was Francisco, gliding through the water so gently that he scarcely rippled the surface as he moved. His hair dripped in ringlets; he stopped swimming and tipped his head back, pulling the curls away from his face.

Jane fumbled in her locker for the nearest suit, a somewhat staid sea-green two-piece that no fashionable woman would be caught dead in. She thought longingly of her clinging maillot, but shook her head and began to dress in the two-piece. She would feel . . . well, *safer* in this.

No one else had stirred; it must be very early, she decided as she padded down the corridor. Her long sleep had refreshed her and the effects of jet lag were beginning to wear off. She was ready for a good hard swim.

Though a rope ladder was slung over the side of the *Fortuna*, she executed a perfect dive into the water, plunging into an aqua world of incomparable beauty. Delicate fans of pastel coral mingled with rolling banners of seaweed. A school of tiny rainbow-hued fish darted away, losing itself in the exquisite beauty.

Jane closed her eyes. She was at home here, at peace, in a way that she had never been above the surface. As the stillness surrounded her, she listened to the beating of her heart, and it seemed to her it matched the subtle movements of the currents that swirled around her.

Reluctantly she surfaced, filling her lungs with spicy air. It smelled of almonds and oranges, of sandalwood and doe-eyed women, their faces framed with lace mantillas. Spain. Where men still fashioned themselves *conquistadores*, where they kept their women like princesses in ivory towers. . . .

"*Buenos días.*" Francisco came up beside her. His skin was the color of toasted coconut, his broad chest matted with thick black hair. The sun glanced off the medal around his neck. He wore a skimpy European bikini, cut so low that she could see the jutting of his pelvic bones above the royal-blue material. A line of curls trailed from his navel inside his suit.

"*Buenos Días,*" she replied, forcing herself not to stare at him. He was so handsome, so wonderfully made, she thought.

And then she caught the same glint of interest in his eyes. He was eyeing her breasts, her firm abdomen, the modest expanse of cloth that covered the lower half of her body. Feigning a casualness she didn't feel, she swam a few paces away. "The sea is lovely."

He bowed his head. "Thank you," he replied, as if he owned it. "Below us, somewhere, lies my treasure."

Her clear eyes widened. "Really? Here?"

"Not quite here, but we are very close. Today we shall begin sweeping with the magnetometer. I know she lies beneath me. I can feel her."

His words made her cheeks burn, her body thrill. If he spoke this way about a ship, how would he treat a woman?. .

"Come. Let's swim." He dived beneath the surface, obviously expecting her to follow. She did, streaming into the magical world of sponges and fishes, then pushed herself to catch up with his long, lithe body. He increased his speed; she did the same, until they were racing, dodging the pink coral and the transparent grasses as if they were mounted on leaping horses. They lunged into the air and plummeted back into the depths, giving each other no quarter. And through it all, Jane kept pace with him.

He gestured to her, and she saw that he had found a lovely fan of coral, as lacy as the mantilla of a Castilian *doña*. She nodded to him and they moved on, so close to one another that their bare feet often brushed each other's legs. He pointed to a school of brilliant yellow fish; she showed him a canopy of seaweed fit for the bedroom of the Infanta of Spain.

Again they surfaced, not speaking. The dolphins had disappeared over the horizon, and the boat was far away. Jane felt alive and young and free. It was the water that made her feel this way, she told herself, and not the enigmatic man beside her. As she trod water, moving her hands in the warm blue sea, she tried to peer at him without his seeing. But it was impossible; every time she looked at him, his eyes were boring into her.

Something changed in the air. It was like the whiff of ozone the deer smells before the thunderstorm, like the muffled rumbling before an earthquake. It was Francisco. She knew it at once, from the way he stared at her, from the way his lips parted. He swam toward her, unsmiling, determined and unstoppable.

He was going to collect the kiss that his mechanic had robbed him of. Let him, her body begged her; but, don't be absurd, her mind chided. You don't even know him.

Catching her breath, she disappeared beneath the waves, seeking refuge in the safest world she knew.

Francisco darted after her. She increased her speed, skimming over razor-sharp coral and fighting through beds of kelp. Still he pursued her.

Then his hands were on her and he whirled her around to face him. She could see the flames dance in his eyes, feel her flesh ignite as his fingertips grazed her shoulders, her neck, her hands. Without warning, he crushed her against his hard body and pressed his lips against hers. He opened her mouth with his tongue, slowly, and filled it with his warm breath. His fingers spread across her back, urging her to exhale into his mouth, filling his lungs with their mingled air. Then he breathed into her again, straining against her.

All intentions of fighting him left her. Her body had been right: it was wonderful, incredible.

The sea surged about them; silken strands of seaweed curled around her legs, caressing her even as Francisco's fingers moved to the small of her back, tracing the elastic of her bathing suit, sliding beneath it as he covered her right breast with his palm. All the while, his breath sustained them both in slow, deliberate rhythm.

Stop this, stop this, she ordered herself. She tried to push him away; he held her fast. His fingers moved inside her top, scratching her nipple with a quick, sharp pain that dissolved into a warm heat between her legs. Still he breathed his life into her, lowering her straps over her shoulders and pressing her naked flesh against the hardness of his chest. She began to struggle, like a fish caught in a net, but his body was clamped around hers. Unyielding, unapologetic, he caressed her breasts as the seaweed waved around them like a curtain.

Her hair fanned around her head and he grabbed long strands of it, twisting it around his fist. Still they breathed together, slowly in, slowly out. Jane felt herself stiffen and then melt, lost in a riptide of desire. The harder she tried to fight against it, the more surely it pulled her down.

Francisco tugged at the buttons of her suit. She cried out, the sound lost in the sea, lost between his lips as he gave her air. His hand gripped her partially exposed flesh and she began to protest in earnest, pushing her palms against his chest. His fingers dug into her soft flesh, clenching when she tightened her muscles against his invasion.

Then slowly they rose to the surface. The shock of the air called her to herself, and she thrashed in his grasp. Gasping, she fought to pull out of his viselike embrace. His lips found her cheeks, the arch of her neck, the soft, sensitive skin beneath her earlobes as she shook her head wildly.

"Do not fight me, *querida*," he murmured. "Do not fight me."

"Let go! I've changed my mind!"

His mouth closed over hers once again. A wave gentled over them as they bobbed in the water. Her body began to explode with a frenzied passion she hadn't known she was capable of. In spite of her struggles, her flesh begged him to stay, to take. To conquer. To dominate.

Not dominate! her mind protested. Not me, not him!

Yes, oh, yes, her body answered. Please, yes.

"Jane," he groaned. "*Por Dios*, how I want you! Juanita, Juanita!"

"No," she breathed, but she knew in that moment that she could fight him no longer. Surrender was too sweet, too exquisite.

Her head fell back in the water as he wrapped his hands around her shoulders. She felt his stomach tighten as he caught his breath. He drew his tongue along her neck, hoisting her in his arms until the water lapped beneath her breasts, exposing the round pink flesh and rosebud nipples.

"Beautiful. *Hermosa.*" His voice was low, hoarse with desire. Breathing harder, he circled her breasts with his tongue, and Jane moaned. More, she wanted to tell him. Please. More.

Then his long, rough man's hands found her bathing suit bottom again, and he began to finish what he had begun beneath the sea. As her last defenses were being stripped away, she came suddenly to an awareness of her vulnerability. She must not do this, she told herself. As Francisco had said, this was business, not pleasure. Nothing but trouble could come of becoming involved with him.

"No, Mr. . . . Francisco," she managed. "Please, I mean it. This—I . . . I don't know you."

"Liar," he said huskily. "You know, *mi amor.* You know."

Suddenly there was a noise from the ship.

Jane's eyes widened. "Oh, God!" she cried. "They can see us!"

"No. We're too far away. They can see nothing," he soothed.

"No!" She wriggled out of his arms and began to swim toward the boat, adjusting her suit as she went.

He didn't go after her. "Swim away, little mermaid," he called. "You can't go far."

Chapter Three

❧

Jane pulled herself up the rope ladder and bounded, dripping, onto the deck. Acutely aware that Francisco was watching her, she deliberately slowed her movements to show that she was unaffected by the passion that had erupted between them.

She was so busy concentrating on her casual pose that she crashed headlong into Carlos, who was bent over his shoe. Startled, he stood before she had a chance to jump back. His bald head nicked her chin, and she stumbled backward.

"*Perdón!*" he cried, catching her arms.

"I'm all right, really," she assured him in English. Then, smiling and nodding to prove it, she veered around him and hurried to her cabin.

"*Ay, maja,*" she heard him whisper. His tone was low, appreciative, and she had the feeling that he had just complimented her.

But she wasn't in the mood for flattery just now. She felt . . . Oh, she didn't know how she felt! Elated and shaken and angry all at the same time. Her lips still tingled from Francisco's kisses; her body pulsated with the pleasure from his hands. And her pride reminded her that this was the male chauvinist who had told her to read *The Taming of the Shrew!*

Hurrying down the ladder to her cabin, she thought of the way she had clung to him, of the hungry need he had elicited in her, and of the desire that had threatened to catapult her into surrendering her body to a stranger. And worse, the stranger was Francisco Pontalba, a man whose opinions of women belonged in those illuminated manuscripts she had seen in the cathedral in Valencia.

Francisco. She had called him by his first name to his face. It was an exotic name, with the subtly rolled R. A name that didn't belong in her world. Could she go back to calling him Captain Pontalba? It would be awkward, after what had passed between them.

And what had? she pressed, pulling off her suit in the confines of her cabin. Nothing. a brief interlude between a sexy Latin and a liberated lady from America. Nothing the manager of Burton Diving School couldn't handle. For heaven's sake, she had fended off worse come-ons than this one!

Worse? Had it really been so bad?

She pulled on a pair of San Diego State track shorts over cotton bikini panties and searched for a bra. Her small breasts jiggled as she bent over, and she thought of Francisco's hands on them, of the way he had kissed them.

The door opened. Whipping her head up, she covered herself as best she could with a pastel green tank top.

Francisco stood in the doorway, his sweatshirt concealing his trunks. His hair was tousled and his feet were bare. He chuckled, leaning lazily against the doorjamb as he surveyed her.

"You're a little girl after all," he said, drawing the door behind him. "You know, Spaniards believe that American women are horribly promiscuous. And very sexy."

"Get out of my cabin!" she cried, then remembered the others and lowered her voice. "Please. I'm dressing."

"I can see that. Don't let me stop you." He folded his arms across his chest and eyed her.

"Mr. Pontalba . . ." She reddened. "Francisco, please. I . . . What happened . . . well, it shouldn't have. Let's just forget the whole thing."

He laughed richly. The resonant sound made Jane's pulse quicken.

"What happened was meant to happen. And your passion

is impossible to forget. You're the kind of woman who enjoys pleasure in a man's arms. And I know much of pleasure.'' His eyes flared as he advanced on her.

She started to back away, but stopped and held her ground. It was high time he learned that she was not a little girl; she was a mature woman, and she wouldn't allow him to toy with her as he might some docile Spanish lady.

''Why don't you let me dive with you?'' she asked abruptly, changing the track of the conversation. It brought him up short.

For a moment he said nothing. His dark eyes raked over her scanty clothes, the tank top barely covering her breasts as she struggled with it. Yearning rose in his eyes.

''And what if I say yes?''

She raised her chin. ''I would appreciate it very much.''

He chewed his lips thoughtfully, and she saw something flicker across his face. Sadness? Disappointment? Frustration? She couldn't tell.

He moved closer, dropping his hands to his sides. ''How much?''

Her lips parted in surprise. He thought she was offering, that she would . . .

Before she could speak, he shook his head. ''No, I won't permit you to dive. I don't have time to watch over you!''

Jane held the top tightly around her. ''But you saw how well I can swim!''

''Yes, I have seen . . . many things.'' Before her eyes, his expression changed. The teasing smile was clouded by a haunted frown tugging at the corners of his eyes and creasing his brow. Then, just as quickly as it had appeared, it faded away.

He gestured toward the pale green material stretched across her chest. ''Don't wear that on board, unless you want all the men to gawk at you as if were a whore.''

With that, he turned and walked out of the room.

Jane stared after him, speechless. Her cheeks burned. A

whore! He had his damn nerve! If he thought she'd stand for his insults, then—

Easy, easy, she cautioned herself. After all, this was a foreign country, with different customs and values. He was not an American. But still . . .

Sighing, she hooked her bra in place and rummaged through her meager wardrobe in search of something more modest. She smiled faintly when she found her "Burton School of Diving" shirt. As if that would impress him. She could be Olympic material and he would wave her away like a bothersome gnat in his superior male way. He certainly hadn't thought she was bothersome a few minutes ago!

But naturally not. After all, wasn't sex one of the few things women were good for?

She buttoned the white shirt and laced her tennis shoes. The aroma of coffee wafted toward her and she heard voices heading for the galley. Breakfast. Her stomach growled petulantly, chiding her for eating so little at dinner.

Squaring her shoulders, she prepared to go topside. She wasn't afraid of him, she told herself. He couldn't throw her off the boat and he couldn't exactly force himself on her, could he? She doubted that even he was that medieval!

The sun sparkled on the azure water. Water birds circled the boat, cawing for a few scraps. In the midst of this serenity, the men of the *Fortuna* were awakening and readying for the first day of the hunt. There was anticipation in the air, eagerness, as if they had caught the scent of their quarry. A few of them were carrying mugs of *café con leche* and plates of rolls toward the awning, chatting and laughing. They nodded their heads at her as she headed toward the galley, still frosty, still resentful.

Only Carlos smiled. He rubbed his bald head, which glistened in the sunshine. "*Buenos días*," he greeted her. "*Se vi nadando*."

Jane worked through the sentence. Her face lit up. "You

saw me swimming!'' she cried. Then her face fell. Swimming—
and what else?

"*Muy bien*," he continued. *Fuerte*." She was strong.

"*Gracias*," she said feelingly. After their history, this was
real progress. Maybe Carlos would help persuade Francisco
to let her join the group.

He pointed to the scuba diver, the school logo, on her
shirt. "You?" he asked in English. She nodded. He took a
sip of his coffee and pointed to the galley. "Ricardo."

Ricardo had coffee ready. Jane thanked him for telling her.
Good grief, she was communicating with him better than she
was with Francisco, who spoke perfect English!

She caught herself. That wasn't exactly true. She and
Francisco had spoken another language out there in the water.
The language of love. . . .

Don't be ridiculous, Jane Marie! she warned herself as she
accepted an earthen mug from a whistling Ricardo. That little
episode had had nothing to do with love.

Brooding, she took her thick, creamy coffee to the encampment beneath the awning. Carlos rose and gallantly offered
her a place beside him on a wooden crate.

"*Gracias*," she murmured, seating herself. One by one,
the others joined them. They still ignored her, until Carlos
told them of her prowess in the water, punctuating his rapid
Spanish with gestures of various swimming strokes. Most of
them shrugged and ate their breakfast, but Ernesto listened
and favored her with a friendly wink.

"*Muy* good!" Carlos enthused. Ernesto chuckled and said
something in Spanish. Ramón guffawed. Jane nibbled at her
roll, her nerves thawing as smiles and laughter surrounded
her. They were beginning to accept her.

Suddenly Francisco stomped up and wrapped his hand
around her shoulder, gripping her so tightly that she almost
spilled her coffee. His lips were pursed, and his eyes flashed
with anger, lightning against black clouds.

"If you please, *señorita*," he hissed. Before she could

reply, he hoisted her to her feet and marched her toward the far side of the galley. He was quivering with rage.

As soon as they were out of earshot, he whirled her around to face him. "And to think I warned you about what to wear! I should have told you how to act! There you sit, smiling at Ernesto and Carlos while they insult you!"

"They weren't insulting me!" she said indignantly. "They were only being friendly!"

"Being friendly? *Hostia, niña*, they were leering at you! You American women astound me! How can you provoke men the way you do, and then act as if they're to blame when they respond?"

"Provoke?" She stared at him. "You must be crazy!"

"No. I'm Latin. I know what my countrymen think of women who smile and laugh too easily. Who allow strange men to kiss them."

Her face drained of color. She stared at him, humiliation spreading through her. The implication was quite clear: whatever he was accusing them of, he too was guilty. He thought the same of her. He thought she was an easy American, ripe and ready. There had been nothing more to his kisses than that.

And so what? she asked herself defiantly. What did she care?

"I see," she said, turning to go.

He grabbed her arm. "You see nothing, Juanita! Nothing!"

"Let go of me." Her voice was like ice. She had never felt so cold in her entire life. It was like plunging into a frozen lake.

With a sigh he released her. "If you were my woman, I'd—"

"But I'm not," she snapped. "Excuse me. I'll finish my breakfast with my *friends*."

"You're being foolish," he told her. "You'll regret this."

"I don't think so, Mr. Pontalba."

She walked away. I won that round, she thought smugly. I bested that man, so sure of himself!

Then she wondered at the empty, hollow feeling in her heart. Yes, she had won, but she also had the strangest feeling that she had also lost.

They spent the morning motoring, dragging the magnetometer behind them in the wake. Francisco hunched over the sensors, straining for the smallest signal from the torpedo-shaped baton, indicating that a large mass of metal had been discovered. For hours he didn't move, only grunting orders in a harsh, preoccupied voice. Pairs of men in scuba gear took turns scouring the bottom for large coral masses, for lumpish forms—anything that might be the rotting hulk of *El Corazón*.

Jane watched him, his back toward her, his shoulders tight with tension. He wants this so badly, she thought, and she found herself forgiving him for his harshness of the morning. Though she itched to join the hunt, she kept silent, occupying herself with helping Ricardo in the galley and trying to help him with his English. Once Francisco appeared, requesting a glass of orange juice, and his voice was so flat that Jane almost asked him if there was bad news. But he disappeared into the navigation cabin without a single word or glance in her direction.

The long day wore on. The *Fortuna* cut through the glassy sea slowly, halting whenever the divers lagged too far behind. Finally Jane went to Francisco. She chose to forget his insults and his advances, ignoring the memories of those tightly clenched hands as they had been on her body, those pursed lips relaxed in the exploration of the sensitive skin of her breasts.

When he heard her enter the cabin, he turned around in his chair. "*Sí?*" he asked sharply. Then he saw her, and his features softened. It was like watching the first streaks of sunlight pierce the morning fog.

"How's it going?" She moved to his side, glancing at his

chart. It was marked with red letters and circles. A compass and straightedge lay beside the chart, and next to them, a pocket calculator. The old tools of the sailor beside the new.

Keeping his face bland, he shrugged. But she saw the tense lines around his eyes and mouth. It couldn't be going too well, considering his mood.

"Let me help," she blurted. "I want to go down."

"No. No diving." His voice was firm; he didn't even look at her as he turned his attention back to the chart. Reaching into a drawer, he drew out a sheaf of aerial photos.

"Please," she pressed. "You know I can do it—"

"No!" he bellowed, his fist smashing down on his desk. "I won't allow it!"

The violence of his refusal stung her. Did he really think she was helpless?

He must have read her mind. "This is not a pleasant swimming pool, you know," he said. "We are not spending Alejandro's money on a lark. This is my life, Jane. And death is . . ." He trailed off. "You cannot dive. I don't wish to hear any more about it."

She scowled at him. "You're really too much," she said in a voice edged with frustration. "In the States, you'd be considered a throwback to the Dark Ages."

"And here, you are too bold." he countered, pushing the photos away and leaning back in his chair. "We are in my country now. We live by my rules."

"I'm not accustomed to living by anybody's rules but my own," she retorted, disconcerted by his sudden intensity. He had that gleam in his eye which she was getting to know quite well. It was like an instinct, the preparatory move toward capturing her in his arms. Almost without realizing what she was doing, she backed away.

He rose. "You're a puzzle to me, Juana Burton," he said slowly. "One I must piece together, bit by bit, until I know the answer to you. And I will do it, before the hunt is over."

His smile was languid. "The hunt. I enjoy it. Don't you?"

Her eyes flashed. "I'm not predatory by nature," she said airily, fighting against the current of erotic tension that was beginning to fill the cabin.

"Sweet lies," he whispered. "*Mentiras.*" His gaze raked her body and she felt naked before him.

"I'm going now," she said unnecessarily. She hurried toward the door.

"There's nowhere you can go that I can't follow." He picked up his red pencil and rolled it between his fingers.

"My misfortune," she snapped.

"Is it?" He regarded her. "I don't think so. As they say, 'Methinks the lady protests too much.' "

"Don't count on it, Don Juan." With a toss of her soft brown hair, she walked out of the cabin and down the hall.

And far enough away to blot out the sound of his laughter.

A while later, Francisco emerged, clad in nothing but the brief triangle of royal-blue material that seemed to be designed to call attention to his tight, hard buttocks and the long, well-defined muscles of his legs. A weight belt was slung low on his small hips, and he set about strapping a knife to his calf. Ernesto appeared, already attired in full scuba regalia. He was carrying a regulator, mask, fins, and air tanks, and handed them one by one to his boss as Francisco prepared to dive. Like a page and his knight arming for battle, they spoke little. Both were intent, so busy with the preparations that neither saw Jane. She sat on top of the galley, knees drawn under her chin, watching. Envy swam in her blue eyes, and anger too, at being forced to remain behind.

At Francisco's sign, the boat engines were cut. Then Francisco gave Ernesto a nod and jumped into the water. Ernesto followed soon after, and the two disappeared beneath the surface.

Jane sighed and climbed down from her perch. Ricardo hailed her from the galley porthole.

"How d'you do!" he called. She managed to smile, and walked over to peer into the open porthole, set high in the bulkhead. She had to stand on tiptoe in order to reach it.

"Fine, thank you, and you?" she asked, prompting him.

"Good. I am good." She applauded and he bowed like a bullfighter, doffing an imaginary matador cap. Why couldn't Francisco be this kind? she wondered. Ricardo was so even-keeled, so unassuming.

But then he wouldn't be Francisco, the mercurial leader, the imposing pirate. The ardent pursuer. . . .

She flushed, recalling her last encounter with him. He was all of those things, and more. Impossible, irascible . . . irresistible?

"Can I help you cook?" she asked hopefully. She had promised to speak to Ricardo exclusively in English so that he could impress his cousin next time they met.

He cocked his head, not understanding. She pointed to the galley and made a stirring motion with her hands. "Do we cook?"

"Ah." He scratched his chin, preparing his answer. "No. We no do. I *siesta*."

"Oh, you're going to take a *siesta*," she echoed, as a pleased smile broke out over his face. "I guess I will too. I'll work on my tan." She pointed to the sun, then to her arms.

He shrugged, a sheepish smile crossing his features. "I to *siesta*," he said. "I do, yes."

"Yes. I'm going to take a siesta in the sun."

Still he didn't appear to comprehend. He laughed and held out his hands.

Chuckling, she wagged an admonishing finger at him. "Patience."

"Ah, *paciencia*," he replied. "I do. You. You do."

"I'm trying to be patient," she sighed. "Old thoughts die hard, I suppose. But your boss is living in the Middle Ages."

Ricardo's face was blank. Of course he hadn't understood

a word. She wouldn't have spoken aloud if she thought he would.

"American," he began. "Don Francisco, *paciencia*. Cousin . . ." He sighed, frustrated by their language barrier.

Jane held up her hand. She wasn't particularly eager to hear about another one of Francisco's *cousins*.

"Sleep well," she said. "I'll see you later."

He bobbed his head. "S'ya later, you."

She found a place on the bow and unbuttoned her shirt until she could tie the ends into a knot across her midriff. The sun was so gold, sparkling like squiggles of glitter in the water. Settling her head against the bulkhead, she squinted at it, sighing, wishing the dolphins of the morning would bound across the horizon. She had a long afternoon ahead of her. It was so ridiculous, his insistence that she not dive. But she supposed that was the Spanish way. . . .

It was hard to know what was Spanish and what was just Francisco. Could you separate a man from his culture? She toyed with a line and picked at the frayed end of the nylon. What was his culture? She knew so little about it, about him. Were Spanish men all so imperious? Ricardo didn't seem that way. But then, he might be with his family, bossing around his wife and his eight children. Did Francisco have a family? Had he learned how to treat women from an aristocratic father who was stern with his mother? Did he ever wonder if his way was right?

She snorted. That, she doubted very much! Francisco Pontalba might question the actions of other men, but she was certain he never questioned his own, especially where women were concerned.

The sun grew hot against her face. Yawning, she closed her eyes. I'll probably dream about him again, she thought, lulled by the bobbing of the boat upon the waves.

She did. As the sun beat down, she dreamed of pirate ships and pieces of eight glinting in torchlight, and of a man who came for her in the moist darkness of the night. . . .

* * *

"You idiot! You're as red as a *gamba*!"

Jane's eyes flew open. Francisco stood over her, still decked in his scuba gear. Bending down, he scooped her into his arms and began to carry her toward the center deck. Water trickled from his hair and rolled down her chest.

"Put me down—ouch!" she gasped. She stared down at her stomach. It was scarlet. She was sunburned from head to toe.

"The sun is very intense," he said needlessly. She winced as he stepped over a coil of rope on the deck.

"You can put me down," she grumbled, furious with her body for betraying her anger at him. Her heart was thudding; her flesh burned hotter than the sunburn where his body touched it. "After all, my feet aren't burned."

He said nothing more. His fingers pressed into the backs of her legs, carefully avoiding her poor, flaming skin. He smelled of the sea, of salt and the secrets of the world below them. She longed to lean her head against his thick chest and breathe in the heady bouquet, but she strained away from him at an awkward angle. Still, his breath wafted against her cheek like the gentlest of kisses. She closed her eyes against the tumult that he was causing. A thousand chills skittered up her spine, a million electric sparks as he shifted her in his arms and looked down at her.

Such eyes. She had never seen anything like them, black fires that danced beneath his hooded lids. The mirrors of the soul, they were said to be, and yet she could see nothing of his soul in them, nothing but passion and striving and conquest.

They reached the ladder. Reluctantly he set her down, his eyes never leaving her face. Averting her gaze, she moved down it painfully, every movement setting a new part of her on fire.

He followed her, taking her up in his arms once more when he reached the bottom. She began to protest, but she saw that he would brook no opposition. One of his hands brushed her knee, and she winced in pain.

"*Lo siento,*" he murmured. "You must be in agony."

Reaching the end of the corridor, he made an abrupt turn to the right and began to open the door.

"It's cooler in my room," he explained. "The port side of the boat has been in the sun all day."

"But—" She winced again and let out a slow breath. "All right."

His cabin was a bit larger than hers, dominated by a desk cluttered with photographs and maps. A coffee cup weighted down a handful of photocopied documents. Several books were piled on top of the chair, with titles in Spanish and French. They all had something to do with oceans, as far as she could tell.

Carefully he laid her on his rumpled bed, moving aside a pair of shorts and his "Universidad de Salamanca" sweatshirt. It was nothing more than a cot, like hers, stiff beneath her back.

"How long did you lie out?" he asked her, unhooking his weight belt and laying it on the floor next to a pair of worn leather sandals. Then he bent down and unfastened his knife. The hair on his lean legs was dark and curly, ending in little wisps on his arches and toes. She had trouble keeping her eyes off him.

"I started just after you left," she replied. Her lips were swollen and sore.

Francisco shook his head. "This is the kind of thing I feared would happen," he muttered, disappearing into the corridor.

"It could have happened to anybody," she shot back, but he was already gone.

Within minutes he returned, carrying a bowl of water and a white cloth. "This will help to cool you."

Setting the bowl by the bed, he pulled over the chair and

sat down. Then quite matter-of-factly he began to unbutton her shirt.

She grabbed his wrists. "Hey, just a minute! I thought I made it perfectly clear that I'm not—"

"Juanita," he said tiredly, "let go of my hands." She tugged at him with all her might, fingers grasping at his well-developed wrists. In one swift move he gathered both of her hands together and jerked them above her head. Needles of pain shot through her.

"You're hurting me!" she cried.

"Then lie still. *Por Dios,* you'd think I was going to rape you." He parted the shirt and clicked his teeth with his tongue. "You should be more careful, *maja.* Your skin is fair, and the sun is a harsh master."

Still restraining her, he dipped the cloth in the water and squeezed it with his left hand. Then he began to daub her skin lightly, gently, allowing it to trickle down her forehead and over her parched cheeks. He moved lower, pressing the cloth with infinite care over her neck, her collarbones, the tantalizing roundness of her breasts as they swelled out of her bra.

He stopped, his grip on her poor arms relaxing. He said something in his lilting Spanish in a seductive, urging voice as he pressed the rag just below her breasts.

His words, husky, wanting, sent a jolt through her body. He must know that he was driving her crazy, in spite of her pain. The slow, feathery caresses, the piercing looks—only a woman made of ice could resist them. And the eyes of Francisco Pontalba would thaw such a woman in no time at all. . . .

He moved the healing coolness down her abdomen, blotting gently. Jane watched his hand, brown against her pinkness, memorizing every detail. There were traces of hair at the knuckles, and a scar in the crevice between his thumb and forefinger which jagged toward his wrist, and his nails were trim and white. That hand had ruthlessly crushed her against his rock-hard body, and now it lay gently against her, mindful of her hurts.

Raising the elastic waistband of her shorts, he rolled the fabric down until the paler skin was exposed. Jane started, but he merely daubed the border of the sun's damage.

Then his careful hands patted her legs. When at last he finished, he opened one of the desk drawers and produced a brown plastic jar with a black lid. "And now, the magic," he said, smiling. "An old home remedy." He unscrewed the lid and held the jar under her nose. The lotion inside was white and smooth and smelled faintly of lilacs.

"What is it?"

He coated the tips of his fingers with it and eased it over her arm. "Something my mother makes for me. Every time I go to sea."

"Your . . . mother?" she managed, undone by the slow, gentle stroke that trailed from her fingertips toward the inside of her elbow, then to her shoulder. All she had to do, she realized, was reach up and pull him down to her. They were both almost naked; it would be such a simple thing. . . .

And then he would think he was right about her, she thought bitterly. That she was an easy American. That she did protest too much.

"*Sí*, my mother," he said, dipping his fingers into the cream. A new warmth glowed in his black eyes. "She's a saint. She can cure anything. In our old place, in Madrid, she was the closest thing we had to a doctor. She's brought dozens of babies into this world, and prevented quite a few from leaving it before their time."

He began to work on her other arm, his elbow lightly grazing her breasts as he reached across her body. She fought the urge to arch her back against his arm. Instead, she watched the expert way he applied the fragrant lotion.

"You're from Madrid?" she asked, out of both curiosity and a need to distract herself from what his nearness was doing to her.

Nodding, he moved to her legs. "Yes."

"But why weren't there any doctors? That's a big city, isn't it?"

His fingers paused on their tantalizing way to her inner thigh. The people were very poor," he said simply. "It was Mama or no one."

"Oh." She swallowed as his hand stole inside her track shorts. The soft folds of her femininity began to pulsate, to pout for his touch. The hard tips of his fingers brushed the curly hair, then moved away. Jane closed her eyes against the wild stabs of erotic longing that plunged through her, forcing herself to breathe steadily, not to give away her weakness.

"Juanita," Francisco whispered. "*Ay, mi amor,*" Her lips flickered; her sore lips parted in a pant.

Then he pressed the cloth against her track shorts and squeezed; the cool water seeped through the material and eddied in rivulets between her legs, caressing her like taunting fingers. She caught her breath and her eyes flew open.

"I told you that I know much," he said huskily, "of pleasure." He bent over her, cupping her right breast with his hand. "I know much of you."

There was a sharp rap at the door.

"Don Francisco! Don Francisco!" The voice was shrill with excitement.

Francisco shouted something in return. But the voice was insistent. As he listened, Francisco's eyes widened. An elated smile broke across his face.

"We have something," he told her, rising from the bed. "*Por Dios,* we have something!"

He threw on his sweatshirt and spoke in rapid Spanish. "I'll come back soon," he promised. "Stay here."

"Is that an order?" she flung at him, stung that he would exclude her from the excitement, and embarrassed, too, that she had fallen so completely under his sexual spell. Now he would be sure she was a promiscuous American, easy prey for a "Latin lover" like him!

He looked surprised. His features hardened. "You never let up, do you, *Ms*. Burton? Yes, it is an order. And see that you follow it!"

With that, he shut the door behind him. Jane stared at the empty space for a long time. Then she rolled over on her stomach, ignoring the pain, and struggled to quell the fires of anger, confusion, and desire that threatened to consume her.

Chapter Four

They didn't find anything that day, nor the next. A week passed. The men began to watch the cylindrical magnetometer with supplicating eyes, as if they were praying to a saint. The *Fortuna* carried an extra cargo of strained hopes and anxiety that weighted her down in the recalcitrant, ungiving Mediterranean.

Where is it? they begged the magnetometer. Where are the crucifixes set with rubies, the tiaras of topazes and emeralds? Where are the silver bars, the golden ropes? Where? Where?

Eight magnificent sunsets had emblazoned the sky since the scene in Francisco's cabin. Jane kept her distance, her nerves taut as she alternately prayed for gold with the rest of the crew and for an antidote to the heady spell Francisco had cast on her.

He was everywhere, circling her, watching her, like a seabird waiting for the ripple that betrays a fish's hiding place. When she lost herself in talking to Ricardo, struggling to break the language barrier, she would turn and find Francisco listening to her. In the twilight, mesmerized by the beauty of the dying day, she would feel his eyes on her back. Sometimes she thought she heard him outside her cabin door, pacing and waiting, stalking her like a wild animal after tender, vulnerable prey.

"But I'm not vulnerable," she mumbled, cleaning shrimp for Ricardo and dropping them into a pot of water. She wiped her hands absently on her Micky Mouse T-shirt and tossed her ponytail out of her eyes. Not to a Latin lover like *el jefe*! It was ludicrous to think that his advances were affecting her, an independent, modern woman! Ridiculous! Back home, she'd laugh in his face if he came on like this.

Particularly when she considered the other side of his treatment toward her. He still forbade her to dive, to help in any way except maybe to check the air lift for holes or refill the crew's air tanks. The man came up from their diving shifts pasty-faced and drained, but he wouldn't allow her to take on some of their burdens. No matter how many times she asked, the answer was always the same.

She knew he thought she was so insistent because she was a bold American woman, unused to deferring to the exalted dictates of men. Many times she had thought about explaining her predicament—that she was hopeful of finding the treasure too, because she needed it to keep the school going. If they didn't find anything, there would be no compensation for her absence during the diving season. Leaving Chuck in charge was a big sacrifice, one that preyed on her.

But no doubt Francisco would merely point at the financial trouble of Burton Diving as a perfect example of her innate inferiority. And he still wouldn't let her go down. She knew him enough to know that.

So why was she so drawn to him? It made no sense. On the contrary, she would be repulsed!

Maybe it was the beauty of the Mediterranean that was stirring her blood. Or the white-washed villages on the islands, sparkling in the sun like monuments to the past glories of Spain. Or the pristine beaches, heady with the scents of pine and cedar, wine and almonds. Or perhaps it was because he was always so close by, so impossibly near. . . .

As if on cue, Francisco stuck his head in the door. He wore a pair of tight cutoffs and a damp T-shirt that clung to his chest.

"Ricardo?" His eyes found her. "*Hola*, Jane. I see you're keeping busy."

Mercilessly she peeled away the crackly shell and picked up the deveining knife. "Oh, yes, Captain Pontalba. As busy as a bee."

"May I trouble you for a glass of sangría?" He looked tired and worried, yet he grinned hugely when she slammed down the knife and reached for the earthen jug of fruited wine that Ricardo had prepared before leaving Jane in the galley to clean the shrimp.

"You have a great capacity," he drawled, "for staying angry at me."

"It's not difficult." She handed him a glass. Chunks of oranges and lemons bobbed in the burgundy-colored drink, like little sailboats on a sea of wine. He tipped his head back, then licked his lips and sighed. He grinned at her chest.

"Disneyland. I've always wanted to go there."

She shrugged. "It would probably be too tame for you." A pink flush crawled up her neck and spread across her face. She hadn't meant to sound so flippant. But it was true—it would be too tame for him.

"I'd be willing to take my chances. I'm an adventurer at heart, you know." He waited to see what kind of effect his words would have on her. She turned back to the pile of shrimp.

"I was enjoying the solitude," she said pointedly.

"Were you?" he murmured, drawing close. "You look so much like my wooden mermaid, standing there with your clenched jaw and steely eyes!"

"She must be a lovely girl," Jane sniped. "I wonder why you want her so badly."

"Because she has so much that I value," he replied, eyes dancing. He was obviously enjoying their sparring match. "She needs to be conqured so badly."

"*El conquistador.*"

"*Exactamente,* Juanita."

"My name is Jane," she said deliberately. "I'm not Spanish. In case you hadn't noticed."

He had no reply. He only stood beside her, following her staccato movements as she attacked another shrimp. He smelled faintly of his mother's cream, and she wondered if he used it to protect his skin. He was very dark, tan as cinnamon, yet he didn't look weather-beaten the way Uncle Chuck did. For some strange reason, it pleased her to think that he took care of himself.

"Do you know the story of *El Corazón*?" he asked. Without speaking, she shook her head.

"*Bueno*, I will tell it to you." Clearing a place on the counter, he perched against it, sipping his wine. His legs, long and lean, were crossed at the ankles, and a scar of white shone on his left shin.

"There were pirates then," he began. "Real ones," he added with a self-deprecatory air. "Not businessmen in fins and masks! They faced unbelievable dangers."

He grew somber. "But then, even today we have danger. Jane, there is a reason . . ." He stopped himself as she looked at him, intrigued. The serious expression disappeared as he scratched his arm.

"We claim to have such a pirate in our family." He laughed. "A corsair. Do you know of them? The Barbary and Maltese corsairs who plundered these waters? The Barbary pirates were Turks, the Maltese, from many countries in Europe." He grinned.

"The Maltese corsairs would board the ships of the Ottoman Empire and navigate them back to Malta or to these islands." He gestured toward the porthole. "The Turks would do the same. It was very confusing, because individual countries and sultanates would make treaties with the enemy in exchange for safe passage across the Mediterranean. No one knew who was an enemy and who was not. So everyone robbed everybody else. Just in case, *naturalmente*."

"It doesn't sound like it was very much fun," Jane said, finding herself warming to the story despite the face that she was struggling to retain her coldness for its narrator.

"Ah, but it was. It must have been glorious! I envy them, Jane. I envy my great-great-many-times-great-grandfather for living then."

Jane cocked her head, studying him. She had not thought he was such a romantic. And she was surprised—and flattered—that he was admitting it to her.

"But they were outlaws," Jane protested mildly, mostly to urge him on. Francisco, she was sure, would have loved to be an outlaw.

"No. In Spain *un corsaro* was as admired as a *conquistador*. He would have fine treasure, many slaves—"

"Slaves!" she cried. "They had slaves?"

"*Sí*. The passengers on the ships they boarded. And they made raids. They would sail right onto the beaches and enslave whole villages." He smiled at her. "Especially the loveliest women."

"How awful!"

He shook his head. "No. Usually the slaves were ransomed. There were clearing houses on Malta and in Turkey for that sort of thing. The Church even got a portion of the money."

He smiled at her shock. "*Bueno*, the story of *El Corazón*. There was a brave Spanish *corsaro*, probably my ancestor, who captured the daughter of a sultan. Her name was Fatima."

"Is this a true story?" Jane asked suspiciously. "Or are you making it up as you go along?"

"Ay, Juanita, of course it's true." He looked wounded. "I read the full account in the archives in Madrid." Flames rose in his eyes. "And I think I was the first ever to do so. The documents were still sealed, *niña*. They crumbled in my hands as I opened them."

She tingled from head to toe. "Sealed? So you think no one else knows of the treasure?"

"No. No one." Their eyes met. For a moment they stared at each other, their excitement the only words they needed. Oh, my God, we really could find it! she thought. It could be ours!

"Fatima," he said finally.

Jane nodded. "The corsair enslaved the sultan's daughter."

Francisco took down another glass and filled it with sangria handing it to her. Her brows arched with mild surprise at his thoughtfulness, but she took the glass he offered and sipped it slowly.

"No. He demanded ransom. She was worth too much to merely enslave her." A flicker of something—surprise? revelation?—crossed his features. He looked at Jane with new eyes.

"Too much to enslave," he repeated slowly, as if puzzled. Studying her, he tapped his finger against his lips, clearly turning something over in his mind.

"Where was I? Ah, so he demanded a fortune. Enough so that he could retire in splendor for the rest of his life."

"The sultan didn't pay up," Jane guessed.

Francisco shrugged lazily and stirred the shrimp, which had been set on the stove. "These are ready to come out now." He began to spoon them onto a towel with quick, dexterous movements.

"No, the sultan was overjoyed that his daughter was alive. He gave *el corsaro* everything he asked for: precious gems, diamonds the size of almonds, over five hundred kilos of gold coins. In return, he demanded the safe return of his child. But a terrible thing had happened in the meantime. Fatima had fallen in love with the *corsaro*. She didn't want to go back. And the poor man couldn't bear to part with her."

"Yes, that is terrible," Jane agreed sarcastically.

Francisco rolled his eyes. "Anyway, they decided to escape to the New World, wild as it was. And still is, if you include Disneyland. *Entonces*, the *corsaro* swore his crew to secrecy; they posed as silk merchants on their way to China. But a storm rose. All hands were lost—Fatima her lover, their treasure. And no one knew, because of the oath of silence."

He paused, staring at her. "They lie at the bottom, in the ruins of *El Corazón*."

Her eyes widened, and she saw that he had advanced on her as he spoke. Ever stalking, he had waited for her to drop her guard. As she took a step backward, her shoulders pressed against the warm bulkhead. Her heart began to pound as his hands rested on either side of her head. They smelled of wine.

"Do you think we should . . . disturb them?" she managed, dizzy. Her blood began to race.

"They are together. That's what they wanted. They have the treasure. That's what I want. That, and something else. . . ."

He bent over her. Their lips met. A brilliant flash shot through her, like the glint of sunlight off newly hammered Toledo steel. I want it too, her body cried out. I want it!

Of their own accord, her arms rose around his neck, pulling him against her. Deep in his throat, he made a growling noise like a regal lion, then pressed her into him, surrounding her with himself.

"Juana, my dove, my light," he murmured, his words running into kisses, like fallen petals floating in a stream. "*Por la Virgen*, I must have your touch! I am your slave, *mujer*, your slave of love."

"Francisco," she breathed. "Francisco, you don't—"

He clamped his mouth over hers, blocking whatever she might have said. A flame blazed through her mind, consuming all thought, even as, in the well of her soul, something tried to whisper to her to pull away, pull away!

But her own need had betrayed her. She hadn't realized how much she wanted him until his lips had brushed hers. For eight days her loins had been smoldering with hunger for him. For eight days she had fought it.

Francisco was the first to move away to bring them both to the reality of their situation. He pressed her cheek against the throbbing vein in his neck. "Not now," he mumbled. "I want it perfect. I don't want you to worry about the others."

As she had the first morning. She squeezed his shoulder, touched that he had remembered.

He roused himself. "And so I will wait. We're going to Mallorca tomorrow, to check the magnetometer. In Mallorca, my heart, we will have each other."

Breathlessly she nodded, loving the feel of him now, anticipating the feel of him then. His maleness pressed against her, tantalizing her with promise.

Doubts scratched at the door of her consciousness, but she forced them away. Not now. The moment was too perfect to cloud with worry and pride.

"Go suit up," he told her, leading her out of the kitchen. "Let's dive."

"What?" she asked, delighted. "You mean scuba?"

Tousling her hair, he laughed like an indulgent uncle. "Yes, I mean scuba. I'll meet you back here in ten minutes. Unless you're a typical woman who takes hours and hours to dress."

"You're impossible!" She laughed, socking his arm. "You win the Oink Award, *Jefe*!"

"No hitting your captain!" He grabbed her hands and held her as she flailed wildly, trying to escape. Her eyes shone as she laughed and fought.

Ricardo turned the corner, then halted as he took in the two of them laughing and roughhousing. *"Buenos días, jefe,"* he said. "How d'you do, Mickey Mouse?" Then he cried out in horror and ran into the galley.

"Mis gambas!" he shrieked. *"Ay!"*

The water on the stove had boiled over. It was cascading onto the floor.

"Oh, God, Ricardo! I'm sorry!" Jane cried, rushing to help him. Francisco caught her hand.

"You are a terrible cook," he teased. She pouted prettily,

loving the relaxed smile on his face. "But a very good kisser."

"And a good diver," she added. "But you'll soon see that."

Jane's heart clutched as the limpid water embraced her, the surrounding glory bringing tears to her eyes. Francisco plunged beside her, streaking past her, then pulled himself up short and captured her in his arms. The bubbles from her tank swirled behind her like a diaphanous gown.

They swam together, holding hands. Francisco pointed to formations of coral and shell-encrusted mounds, gesturing that these were likely hiding places for the ship. She nodded her understanding, sharing his excitement, but also thinking of Fatima and her lost love. She had loved a Spaniard, that lady of long ago. She had been willing to give up everything for him—her family, her country, her very life. Did such love exist in this modern world of magnetometers and motorized boats? Or had it gone the way of galleons and sultans?

Their fingers slid away from each other as Francisco glided ahead, swooping down to peer at some coral farther on. Jane watched his body, so incredibly sculptured, his black wet-suit jacket molding the firm lines of his chest and arms.

Am I doing the right thing? she wondered. Damn, I really went crazy back in the galley! Chills of remembered pleasure rippled up her back. He's changing, she thought hopefully. He must be. After all, he finally asked me to dive with him. . . .

She swam through the beauty of her kingdom—their kingdom, hers and her pirate king's. Past coral and barnacles and spiny anemones, orange and purple flowers of the deep. Mentally she hugged herself. Mallorca. Francisco. It would be all right. It really would.

Francisco was far ahead. She could see him clearly in the glassy water, his fins waving in slow motion as he moved along. Smiling, she prepared to catch up with him.

Below, something glinted at her. She blinked. Gold!

No, it couldn't be. But there it was again!

She glanced back up, trying to catch Francisco's attention. But she no longer saw him. For a moment she debated, wondering if she should go after him to show him or explore further. If she moved, she might lose track of just which inch of sand had winked at her. And there were many, many inches of sand in the Mediterranean.

She could see why treasure hunting could be frustrating, even with the help of advanced technology. The sands shifted, the water moved . . . and what might have been directly in one's line of vision had disappeared in the wink of an eye.

Where was it? She edged around some sharp coral, chuckling when a school of tiny gray fish darted away from her, their tails and fins working like so many miniature outboard motors. She watched their comical retreat, then bent to her task once again.

It was here. No, there! There it was. Fascinated, she dived deeper, checking the pressure gauge on her wrist. She had plenty of air to go deep if she needed to. But where was Francisco? She wished he would come back.

If it were gold, she daydreamed as she swam toward it, surely the men on the *Fortuna* would accept her at last. She'd be the local hero! Uncle Chuck would be so pleased. And Alejandro. But best of all, Francisco would never argue when she asked to join the hunt.

Let it be, let it be, she prayed, pressing on through the water. Please, for me . . .

Something grabbed her around the waist. Frightened, she clutched at it, only to realize they were Francisco's hands. Before she knew what was happening, he propelled them both toward the surface. They flashed through the water like bullets and flew into the air as they broke the surface.

Francisco tore his regulator away. "Damn you!" he thundered, his voice cracking. Behind his mask, his face was pale. "Why did you swim off?"

Jane pulled out her own regulator. "Francisco!" she cried. "I saw gold! I saw it!" She gripped his arms excitedly.

"Damn you!" he bellowed again. This time, she was caught up short by the rage in his tone.

"Were we in some kind of danger?" Jane asked, dazed. "I didn't see anything." His hands were shaking. She had never seen anyone so furious. He raised one clenched fist, and for a moment she was afraid he was going to hit her.

"And you call yourself a diving instructor! Thank God I didn't listen to you! What was Alejandro thinking of, sending you? You know nothing about diving!"

Jane jerked away from him. Rage shot out from him in all directions. She was surprised the water wasn't boiling.

"What are you talking about? I didn't do anything wrong!" Her mind ran through her actions, just to be sure. No, she had followed every rule of diving. Satisfied, she raised her chin and challenged him to point out her error.

"You swam off!" he shouted. "I had no idea where you were!"

"Francisco," she said slowly, amazed, "I only dropped out of sight for a moment. I kept my eye on you. I knew where you were. There was no danger—"

"There is always danger!" He smacked the water with his fist. "Always!"

His eyes blazed. "This was a test, *señorita*. And you have failed it miserably. No diving for you. Not on my time. Not on my hunt."

He began to swim toward the boat. Jane stared after him.

"You're being unfair!" she cried. "You're being unreasonable!"

He swung around to face her. He looked like a coiled spring; ready to unwind. "I don't give a damn," he said in a low, toneless voice. "I am *capitan* here. I don't need to be reasonable. Come back to the *Fortuna*. Now."

"But—"

"Juanita, I am not in the habit of being disobeyed!" he

yelled. "Get on that boat before I drag you there by your hair!"

He waited for her. Warily she began to sidestroke, facing away from him, struggling to regain her composure. Was he insane? He had to be, to fly apart like this over such a simple thing as losing sight of her for a minute. He had only to look around to find her again.

The men of the *Fortuna* were hanging over the railing, eyes agog as she and Francisco swam toward them. Trading grins, they murmured their approval of Francisco's treatment of her. Ricardo, clad in his white apron, wrung his hands like a worried older brother.

Francisco reached the rope ladder first. Glowering at her, he held it taut as she climbed it. With a loud thud, she landed on the deck, as Ricardo came forward to help her with her tanks.

"No," she said firmly. "Thank you. I can manage." Unbuckling the straps, she lowered the barely used tanks to the deck.

Francisco appeared. Wordlessly he began to divest himself of his gear.

"Don Francisco," Bernardo said. He pointed to Francisco's leg. A long cut jagged from the side of his knee toward his ankle. Blood pooled around his foot.

"I cut myself," he muttered in English, "searching for you."

Jane slung her tanks over her shoulder and picked up her fins. "I'm sorry, Francisco. But I saw a piece of gold! I really did!"

"Don't be ridiculous," he snapped, pressing his hand over the wound as Ricardo ran back with the first-aid kit. "We're nowhere in the vicinity of the wreck."

"I know what I saw!" she protested. "Why won't you even consider that I might be right? Because I'm a woman?"

"*Gracias*, Ricardo," he grumbled, wiping the scarlet from his leg as Ricardo looked on. "You know nothing about sunken treasure," he said. "If I swam down to look at every single gleam I saw while diving, I'd waste all my time." His eyes were cold as he glared at her. "We have a budget, you know. Alejandro can't keep financing us forever. Which is one of the reasons I cannot spend my time worrying about you. No more diving. I mean it, Juanita."

With as much dignity as she could muster, she unhooked her weight belt. They were back at each other's throats. The precious moment in the galley was lost forever, like the glittering object she knew she had seen in the water.

"We'll settle this later," he said as she walked past. "When we dock in Mallorca."

"Forget it," she replied, speaking just as icily, just as deliberately as he had. "It doesn't matter."

But of course, it did.

They docked at Mallorca at twilight, in a cove not far from the main harbor, but far enough to keep attention away from their treasure boat.

Tonight they were camping on the beach. The men seemed more relaxed, enjoying the freedom to move where they pleased, and sure that once the magnetometer was checked over, they would find *El Corazón*. In the meantime, they were also going into town to pray for good fortune at the church dedicated to their patron saint, San Pedro.

Layers of rock, as ancient as the sea, pressed together at sharp angles and tilted toward the water. The sand was cool and velvet-soft beneath Jane's feet as she watched the others grouped around a fire, finishing Ricardo's delicious feast of chilled lobster and olives. She sat apart, hidden in the darkness, her heart so heavy it felt as if it were made of lead. Reaching for her sangría, she downed it in one gulp, the bits of fruit bobbing against her upper lip.

Carlos, Ernesto, and Francisco pulled out guitars and began to play. Jane closed her eyes and forced back the hurt, angry tears as she saw that Francisco was patently ignoring her. Tonight was to have been their night of love, and now she was so furious she felt like drowning him.

"Mickey Mouse, hello," Ricardo murmured, holding out a small bowl of sugared almonds.

Jane shook her head. "No, thanks, Ricardo. I'm not hungry."

"*Dulces?*" he asked, producing a frozen Mars bar from his pocket. She gave him a weak smile and took it. As before, her shaking hands prevented her from unwrapping the chocolate. Ricardo closed his fingers around hers and did it for her.

"Come, we do," he said, pulling her to her feet and indicating the beach. The firelight flickered on Francisco's face as he bent over his guitar, the strings crying beneath his fingers as he began a strange, haunting melody. Carlos and Ernesto followed his lead, as the others fell silent to listen.

The music began slowly, a series of gentle strums. Francisco's guitar found its voice and began to sing. There was tension in the song, punctuated by the steady, unbending strums of the other two, and passion. Jane felt her pulses quicken as the rhythm increased. Francisco's eyes were closed; he, too, was feeling the music. It mounted, rising to a new height, a new sense of restrained eroticism.

Then all three guitars broke into a crescendo of emotion, a frenzy of notes as the men's fingers demanded more, and more. The air was a symphony of wild Gypsy song, of abandon, of victory and surrender.

Jane followed Ricardo away from the fire, embarrassed by her fierce reaction. Her body was quivering; she had never been more aware of everything around her, of the smell of the fire and the pines that hovered above her; of the way the ocean rose and swelled with the victorious guitars. The water covered her feet with its warmth as they walked farther on, away from the siren call of the music.

Still they played. Jane peered over her shoulder at the receding campfire. She could barely see Francisco, cloaked in smoke and shadow like the Dark Angel himself, beguiling her with his song of temptation. She thought of Odysseus and how he had his men lash him to the mast to guard against the sirens, whose hypnotic singing lured men to their doom. She had no such protection against Francisco and his guitar.

Except her anger. Dammit, why did he have to be so macho? Why couldn't he believe her capable of anything?

They moved farther into the heady fragrances of the night. The glistening canopy of stars seemed to rise above the milky moon that glowed like the finest alabaster. This was the same sky Fatima had loved beneath, lying in the arms of the corsair who dared to capture her soul and her heart.

Oh, why did everything have to be the way it was? she wondered. Why couldn't she be a woman of that era, unused to anything but repressive men and confined by narrow choices? Back then, women thought of nothing but pleasing their lords and masters. Why did she have to know better? For a moment she almost resented the freedom she had in this modern day and age to be a man's equal and to expect to be treated as such.

Ricardo pointed to a rock, waiting for Jane to sit first. Working his lower lip, he joined her. They were quiet, barely able to hear the guitars above the swell of the waves.

"*Señorita*," he began in a low, serious voice. He turned to her with sad eyes. "Don Francisco, cousin." He sighed. "*Se murió*." He pointed to the water.

"I don't understand." She didn't think she wanted to anyway, if this was a story about yet another one of Francisco's "cousins."

He thought for a moment. "*Muerta*."

"Dead?" That was one word she did understand.

"Cousin, *señorita*, cousin. María," he told her. "María del Carmen Serra y Pontalba. Please, to do." He pantomimed putting on scuba gear. "Don Francisco, cousin."

"They went diving? Scuba?" His eyes glistened.

"*Sí Sí!* Cousin . . ." He continued with his pantomime. It was a tale of terror, one every diver feared. Jane's heart lurched as she followed it—the caught foot, the fast-emptying air tanks, clawing for oxygen, struggling, writhing, receiving help—too late.

Too late. Jane gasped.

"Oh, God! She died! María was diving with Francisco and she died!"

Ricardo closed his eyes and exhaled slowly, aging before her eyes. "*Muerta.* Don Francisco . . ." He pointed at Jane, then at the sea. "You, cousin. You no *muerta.*"

The guitars rose in a wild cry, a sob of pain that volleyed along the beach. "Oh, Francisco," she whispered. "Oh, poor love."

The Mars bar slipped from Jane's fingers and fell into the sand. Tears rolled down her cheeks. Awkwardly Ricardo patted her hands.

"Don Francisco," he said, rapping his fist against his chest.

"I understand." She stared at the tiny point of light that was the campfire. "How long ago did it happen?" Her last name had been Pontalba. His real cousin? Or his wife?

Ricardo cocked his head, shrugging. "I no understand."

"It's all right. I don't suppose it matters. Scars can last a lifetime. . . ."

"You . . ." Pressing his finger against his lips, he indicated that she shouldn't speak of it further. Nodding, she watched as he got to his feet and shuffled away toward the encampment.

The moon moved across the sky, casting glimmers of silver on the far crests, like a painter working on black velvet. Jane lost herself among them, her mind spinning. No wonder he was so adamant about not diving. No wonder he had lashed out at her when they had separated this morning. He was mortally afraid for her.

She would have to honor that fear while she was on his

boat. Though it would be difficult, it was only until the hunt was over. Then she would go back to San Diego and . . .

And try to forget him. Her throat tightened. As soon as they found the gold, she would lose Francisco.

But that didn't matter. Beyond this time together, she could hope for nothing between them. They were from different cultures, different worlds. It would be disastrous.

Then she saw him. Rising from the sea, Francisco's head and shoulders glistened in the moonlight. The Mediterranean surged around him, the curls of hair on his muscled chest glistening in the soft light. A silver sheen undulated on his skin as he climbed in splendor from the sea. His body was perfectly sculptured; he was a bronze Poseidon, come to claim his due.

He was nude. She caught her breath as the sea fell away from him. exposing his hard body to her like a challenge. His masculine form tapered to his small hips, the sharp crevices where bone met muscle, and farther below, the proud evidence of his desire for her.

She thought of his arrogance. She thought of their arguments. She thought of María. And then she went to him.

Sliding off the rock, she walked straight toward him, the warm water rushing over her toes, her ankles, her shins. Her sodden jeans wrapped around her legs, exposing the roundness of her hips and the cleft between her thighs. Her clear blue eyes were intent as she moved with the surge of the surf, drawing nearer and nearer to Francisco.

He cut the space between them in half, then half again, then caught her up in his arms. The first kiss, of reunion, was fierce. The second, of passion, was fiercer still. Jane arched herself against his hot, wet skin, crushing her lips against his as his tongue invaded her mouth. The sweet taste of wine was on his lips; she scattered her kisses to find there was salt along the arch of his neck and the special places behind his ears. Francisco leaned his head back as he held her in the waves, the moon splashing down on his craggy features. Jane pulled his face to hers for another kiss, yet another.

At last he carried her back to the edge of the water, laying her reverently on the sand as the water caressed her, a piece of seaweed wrapped around his hips like a corsair's sash.

He studied her face, kneeling over her as she held out her arms to embrace him. Then his trembling hands learned the bridge of her nose, the hollows of her cheeks, her small, pouting lips. Her back arched; her breath came out all at once in a gasp as his fingers screamed beneath her chin and along her neck, clamping on her shoulders.

His mouth found the taut corners of her mouth, the skin stretched tightly over her cheeks. Moaning, he moved to the wild, throbbing pulse in her neck and fastened there, as if he were a dark vampire of the night, feeding on the boiling blood that roared through her veins.

All the trappings of the modern world fell away, melting beneath the heat of his touch. More than anything, she wanted to be conquered by this man, and in that, to conquer him herself. She ran her fingers down the curve of his back, around his small, firm buttocks, along his chest until she found his rigid manhood.

"*Ay*," he breathed, *ay, mi amor*." He began to murmur in Spanish, a chant of words she didn't know as his hands and lips bewitched her. "Juana."

She helped him undress her, tugging the material when it would not obey her shaking hands. They they lay naked and panting, exploring each other's bodies, straining to make the ecstasy last and last.

"By the Saints, you are beautiful," Francisco gasped, eyes flaming, as he surveyed her. He ran his fingers through her hair, fanning it around her head like a halo. The strands swayed in the water as he picked them up and buried his face in them, then went on to worship her entire body with languid, reverent, yet torturous kisses. The water flowed around her, swirling over her legs and arms, but it did nothing to quench the flames that threatened to overcome her.

Francisco's hands traveled to the hollow of her stomach, palms flattening as he pressed her back into the sand. His hands took her, teasing the soft pink folds of her femininity with knowing, quick fingers, and rolls of pleasure cascaded over her, bursting like fireworks. The sea, the night, Francisco . . . she felt she must go mad with delight.

"Please," she whispered hoarsely. "Oh, Francisco, please!"

"Not yet," he murmured . "Not yet." He ran his fingers along her inner thighs, light, feathery explorations that made her moan with wanting him. He taunted her, tantalized her, denied her even as he gave so much.

"Now," she pleaded again, but he shook his head.

Unable to bear the exquisite torment a moment longer, she pulled away from him, and twisted agilely until she was poised above him, his wrists pinned to the sand by her work-strengthened hands.

"Now," she commanded, reveling in his domination as she took what she had longed for. Francisco caught his breath as he easily freed his arms. His hands wrapped around her waist, moving her to his rhythm as his eyes closed in ecstasy. Jane gloried in the sight of him, matching his rhythm, meeting his thrusts. Her hair brushed his chest as he panted, clenching his teeth to stem the tide of his climax while they battled for a mastery of love.

"Woman, what are you doing to me?" he whispered hoarsely, but she silenced him with a kiss. Her fingers tightened around him and she began to move with all the force of her swimmer's body, her need overcoming her restraint, driving her past Jane and Francisco, past Man and Woman, to the very essence of passion and wanton desire. He thrust into her like a wild thing, caught up in the primitive urges that screamed for more, and for an end. . . .

"Jane!" he cried, throwing his head back in triumph, slamming into her with all his maleness. She was with him; she exploded into a brilliant flash of unimaginable delight that coursed through her like molten lava. I'm dying, she thought incoherently. I'm no longer in the world.

And then she was back, lying atop Francisco, slumped against his salty broad chest. His fingers clutched her tightly, as if she would slip into the sea if he didn't hold her. Jane stared down at his bowed head, the soft, wet hair curling against her neck. Moved, she touched the chestnut strands tenderly.

Francisco stirred, opening his eyes. "My hot-blooded American," he said quietly. "Come and rest beside me."

Jane obeyed, settling herself in the crook of his arm. But she didn't rest. All night she watched the moon shift across the sky, and long before morning, she realized that beside her, Francisco was also awake. His dark eyes caught hers when she turned over, and his lips rekindled their passion.

And this time, it was she who surrendered.

Chapter Five

"Mickey Mouse, how d'you do?"

Jane opened her eyes, shutting them quickly against the brilliant sun. It was big and gold, sizzling on the sand. She felt droplets of perspiration on her brow. A lightweight sheet covered her; beneath it, she realized, startled, she was dressed in a man's green T-shirt and the panties she had worn last night.

Last night. The memory flooded her with pleasure, replaced by embarrassment as Ricardo's shadow hovered over her with a cup of *café con leche*.

"Good morning," she replied in English. "How are you?" Did he know? Did they all know? She raised herself on her elbows and looked around. Bedrolls were propped beside the ashes of the campfire; a tarp had been strung between two pines. Carlos sprawled beneath it, studying a map. Ernesto was chomping on a roll.

Sipping her coffee, she tipped her hair out of her eyes and smiled. "This is good," she told Ricardo. She touched his hand. "Thank you, Ricardo. For telling me about Don Francisco."

Solemnly he nodded. He made a waving gesture, taking in the entire camp. "No one," he said. She understood. They were the only two who shared the captain's secret.

The sheet fell away as she moved, revealing the T-shirt. She caught Ricardo's speculative glance and realized that the shirt was Francisco's and that she wore no bra. Her breasts pushed against the clinging cotton. Ricardo's cheeks reddened. He sat back on his haunches and worked his lower lip between his teeth. Finally his brown eyes crinkled and he smiled as he got up and walked away.

"*Muchachos!*" she heard Francisco call. He stood on the deck of the *Fortuna*, talking to the men, his broad back hidden by his sweatshirt. Track shorts were hiked almost to his hips, revealing his long, lean legs and the small curve of his buttocks. The sun cast a sheen on his dark hair like a crown.

That man had lain on top of her. He had kissed every inch of her nude body, explored the most secret places of pleasure. The very sight of him aroused her.

Self-consciously Jane pulled the T-shirt around herself. They were all there, the others, like a wall between her and Francisco. And they must know that their boss had slept with their American bad luck after only eleven days at sea. Eleven days! She had never done anything like this before in her life.

The breeze ruffled Francisco's hair as he turned toward her. She smiled at him, flushing, trying to gauge his reaction. What were they to each other now?

"Good morning, *señorita*," he said formally. At first she was taken aback, and then she realized that he was probably trying to maintain appearances in front of the crew.

She inclined her head. "Good morning, *señor*. May I come aboard?" she asked in a bantering tone. "I'd like to change my clothes."

He hesitated, his lips pursing in a firm line. "I'll bring some to you," he said. "We're busy right now."

"Oh. Well, I'll just slip into my cabin. I won't cause any—"

"Jane," he cut in, "I don't have time to argue with you. I'll bring you some clothes when I have a minute."

Her eyes widened in surprise at the irritation in his voice. How could this be the same man who had murmured words of love to her in the night? Her body recalled the magic he had wrought, how gentle he had been, but as he stood on the deck, scowling, she could almost believe that she had dreamed the whole thing. Almost.

"All I want is to look presentable," she pressed. "I can't even get out of bed!"

"Hosta!" he snapped. "I said I'd take care of it in a minute! Now, be quiet!"

"Francisco . . ." she began, but there was nothing she really could say. She winced at the soreness in her muscles as she began to wrap the sheet around her like a sarong. Each ache was a reminder of Francisco's touch, of the joy he had given her.

In her pique, she took a step forward and stumbled on her sarong. It fell to the sand, revealing her brief bikini panties and Francisco's T-shirt.

"Maja." The voice was soft, appreciative. It came from the boat.

Francisco whirled on his crew, slashing them with furious Spanish. They shrank back, shaking their heads. Jane understood: no one would own up to the compliment—or insult—whatever in heaven's name Francisco thought it was!

At last Ramón stepped forward with bowed head, shrugging fatalistically as Francisco reprimanded him. Muttering, the man moved away to attend to something at the stern. The others drifted off, casting glances at Jane. Gathering up her sheet, she made her way toward the tarp with as much dignity as she could muster.

Carlos scooted to one side, making room for her on the canvas that lay on top of the sand. He grinned at her, then went on with his map-reading.

Jane sighed, leaning against the base of the pine. In spite of herself, disappointment welled in her heart. She understood his fear for her; she understood his passion. What she didn't comprehend was why he didn't think twice about barking at her and treating her like a pariah when he wasn't trying to make love to her! He was like Jekyll and Hyde—so loving, then so domineering. It didn't make sense.

Then she remembered Alejandro's warning: Francisco would be playing by another set of rules, he had told her. He would assume that she knew how to play the Spanish way too.

Well, she didn't. She didn't even know what the game was.

Her ratty tennis shoes dropped in her lap. A pair of shorts followed. A chambray shirt. Then panties. A lacy bra. Jane snatched her underwear out of sight and glanced up at Francisco. Carlos, she saw, had gotten to his feet and was ambling toward Ricardo.

Francisco's chiseled jaw was clenched and his eyes still smoldered. "You should learn patience," he said stonily. "It will make you seem less shrewish." He held out his hand to her. "Get dressed," he told her. "Emilio Olivetas and his wife will be here soon."

"Who are they?" she asked, wondering how on earth she was supposed to put on her clothes.

"Emilio is an old *compadre* of mine, He's coming to work on the magnetometer." He sighed. "The radio's acting up, too."

"Oh, I'm sorry," she said, touching his hand. "I guess I've been a pest about diving and helping with the hunt. I wouldn't be so stubborn, except that . . ." She stopped, not wanting to burden him with her own worries.

"Something is bothering you?" he asked, as if able to read her mind.

She shrugged. "It's my problem. I mean, it doesn't have anything to do with you."

Straightening her fingers, he brought them to his lips and kissed them. "Still, I want to know." He checked his watch. "Would you like to take a walk?"

Before she could answer, he rose to his feet. "Dress," he said, gesturing to the pine she leaned against.

She was surprised. The others were only a short distance

away. If one of the them took it into his head to walk down the beach or to seek the shelter of the tarp to get away from the sun, he would see her. Yet Francisco seemed unconcerned. He held the branches away as she scooted behind them.

Suddenly she felt shy. The moon had hidden so much from him. It would be quite another thing to stand naked before him in the sunlight.

"*Ay niña*, don't be embarrassed," he said. There was warmth in his voice, an enjoyment in coaxing her.

Lifting her chin, she pulled the T-shirt over her head. Her nipples contracted in the breeze as she stood before him in nothing but her pink underwear. He breathed in quickly.

"So lovely." His voice dropped, husky, intimate. "Now the other." He gestured to her panties. Hesitantly she stepped out of them.

"*Dios*, you move with the seduction of a flamenco danger. You're like molten satin, like the queen of passion. Juanita, I want to take you. I want to feel your skin of silk and flame against me, as I did last night."

She wanted it too. Her hurt feelings were forgotten as she bathed in the warmth from his gaze.

"The men . . ." she said.

Not taking his eyes off her, he nodded. "The men. The magnetometer. The hunt. Would you report it to Alejandro if I took the time to walk with you? Or would you tell him that I was wasting his money?"

She drew back, wounded. "I don't report to Alejandro! I'm just here to reassure him—"

"That I won't steal from him. You know I won't. Unless you belong to him."

"Belong to him! I don't *belong* to anybody!"

"You will," he promised as she zipped up her shorts.

They climbed to the top of the cove, watching the crew scurry over the deck of the *Fortuna*. Francisco frowned as Ramón dropped his pants and urinated over the side of the boat.

"Look away, Jane," he growled.

Her mouth twitched, but she obeyed.

He drew himself up. "In Spain, we do not piss in front of ladies," he informed her.

She couldn't help it. She began to giggle.

Francisco flushed. "Jane, please."

"I'm sorry," she managed. "It was just the way you said it. 'In Spain, we do not piss . . .' " She dissolved into a gale of laughter.

"You shouldn't say that word," he huffed. He sat helplessly as she held her sides and bent forward to muffle her amusement.

"Why not? You did."

"But . . ." He sighed. "This is one argument I can't hope to win. You American women!"

"You Spanish men!" Wiping her eyes, she settled against a rock and allowed herself one last chuckle.

"As I recall," Francisco said, "we came up here to discuss a problem."

"Oh, well, if you're sure you want to listen." She grew serious. "You see, this is the big season for our diving school. And with me gone, it's hard on business."

"But you have your uncle. Surely he could find another assistant for the summer."

Jane held out her hands. "I pretty much ran things. It was more like he was my assistant. To be frank, the school's in trouble. Alejandro offered us a cut in his share of the treasure as payment for my coming with you."

Francisco took this in. "I see. Have you no other male relatives who could help you? Where's your father?"

Jane licked her lips. Somehow she had thought he knew all about her.

"He's dead," she said bluntly. "My parents died when I was ten. Then I went to live with my uncle."

Francisco looked alarmed. "Both of them?"

She nodded.

"Oh, *niña*," he breathed, putting his arms around her. His chin nuzzled the crown of her head. *"Pobrecita,"* he mumured. "Poor little one."

"It was a long time ago," she whispered. "I don't even remember them very well anymore. Chuck's been my family. . . ."

"This uncle who forces you to run the school?"

"He doesn't force me. He's just not any good at it."

"My sweet Jane." He closed his eyes and kissed her forehead. "My Jane."

His hands rested on either side of her face, and for the first time she could remember, she felt utterly safe. Her lids fluttered as she drank in the sensation.

"This is why it's better if women don't work," he said. "In Spain, we protect them from that. We work day and night so that they can take care of their homes and their children."

She stiffened unaccountably, since what Francisco thought of the roles of men and women had nothing to do with her future.

"What if they want to work?"

"They can do charity work," he said firmly. "For the church or the arts. There are orphanages and missions."

"But—"

"Look. Emilio is here." He kissed her cheek. "Juanita, don't worry about the treasure. We'll find it. And later on today, we'll phone San Diego and you can find out how everything is going." He cocked his head. "Why did you tell me about your school?"

She considered. "I guess I was hoping it would make you see that I have a reason for wanting to help so badly. It's not just because I'm a shrew. I don't really want to prove a point." Well, that wasn't exactly so. But she didn't amend her words.

"And I have a good reason for not permitting it," he said softly. "Now, come. Emilio needs me."

*   *   *

Emilio and his wife, Celia, were younger than Jane had expected. Both had raven hair and chestnut eyes, and both were tall and thin. Celia's hair was gathered into a chignon that coiled at the nape of her neck, and she wore heavy makeup and large triangles of silver that dangled from her ears.

Emilio, his hair kinked into a dandelion-style perm, embraced Francisco in the Latin style, then bobbed his head when he was introduced to Jane. Celia gave Francisco a kiss on the cheek.

"*Bueno, mano,*" Emilio said, rubbing his hands together. "Let's find out what's wrong." He turned to Celia. "Come back at five, *querida.* Then we'll take these treasure hunters out on the town!"

"No, Celia," Francisco interrupted. "We'll meet you in town. Jane and I have some errands to run." He smiled at Jane and said something to Celia in Spanish.

"*Bueno.*" she nodded. "At three-thirty, in Café Hortensia."

Jane creased her brow. "I'm sorry. I don't understand. Am I going somewhere?"

Celia clicked her teeth. "Francisco, didn't you tell her? You're to be my guest for today. We're going sightseeing."

Jane frowned at Francisco. "I thought maybe I could help with the repairs. After all . . ."

Francisco gave Emilio a look and said something in Spanish. Then he wagged a finger at Jane. "Don't worry, *Ms.* Burton. Everybody else is going into town, too. The men want to go to Mass. Only Emilio and I are staying behind."

Jane was abashed. "Oh, well, I see." She took in Celia's embroidered gauze skirt and frilly blouse. Bright red toenails peeked from polished leather sandals. "Shouldn't I wear something else?"

Both men laughed. "Spoken like a true woman!" Emilio said approvingly.

"Lend me some money, *hombre,*" Francisco said. "I want to encourage these feminine impulses!"

Emilio handed Jane a sheaf of Spanish bills. "Have fun, you two. Celia, no more shoes!"

"Oh, Emi!" The woman pouted.

"I mean it," Emilio said sternly.

"*Ay*, all right. Come on, Señorita Burton. Let's go!"

Jane tried to hand the brightly colored bills back to Emilio. "I can't take your money," she protested.

"Ah, no, *señorita!* It's Francisco's now."

"Well, then, I'll pay you back," she told *el jefe*. But she didn't want to spend any of her money, either, she thought. She didn't have that much of it.

"No, Juanita. It's yours. Buy yourself something pretty." He touched her cheek, "Something blue, like the water. Then you can wear it tonight. And new shoes, too. Ask Celia to help with those. Celia has more shoes than anyone else on Mallorca. *Verdad*, Celia?"

Emilio's wife laughed airily. "And I saw such a lovely pair in Torrejón's. They were white, and they had the prettiest wooden heels . . ."

Emilio sighed. "One more pair, woman! Then no more!"

Celia clapped her hands together and kissed him on the cheek. "*Gracias, papacito.* Come on, *señorita!* Let's leave before they change their minds!"

The first thing that caught Jane's eye when they came within view of the city of Palma was the cathedral. It glowed in the sunlight like a topaz, golden and warm. Celia smiled and pulled the black Mercedes onto a shopping street bustling with Mallorcans and tourists.

"We can see it, if you like. But first, we will have to buy you a dress."

Jane hesitated. "I don't really want to spend Francisco's money," she said. "And I didn't bring much with me."

"Now, don't feel that way!" Celia reassured her. "Francisco loves to spend money on pretty . . ." She caught herself.

"You must have a souvenir of your journey, no? There are lovely boutiques on the Borne. Come, I'll show you."

They wove through stretches of aged whitewashed buildings, their roofs at odd angles to each other, past modern skyscrapers of concrete and glass. Men often whistled at them or called out in low, suggestive tones. Celia didn't seem to notice at all.

"It must be very exciting," she said at one point, "to be on a treasure hunt with Francisco Pontalba!"

Jane's cheeks warmed. "Yes, it is."

Celia was clearly curious about her, but too polite to say so. "Ah, here is the dress shop that I love above all others!" she cried. "Not too many tourists know of it, so the prices are low. Especially compared to the mainland. Francisco wants you in blue, eh? That's a good choice."

Celia led the way into one of the whitewashed buildings, down a corridor, and into an enclosed plaza. Streamers of brilliant fuchsia and red flowers trailed over the upstairs balconies, reflected in the water of a small tiled fountain.

"Señora Bayeu!" she called, clapping her hands. Her eyes danced. "I have spent enough on Doña Sylvia's clothes to finance two treasure hunts! Thank God that I have a husband who indulges me!"

Before she knew what was happening, Jane was decked out like a queen. Her new blue dress was exactly the color of the Mediterranean, a vivid blue that showed off her trim, athletic body to perfection. The thin straps of sapphire-silk cord accentuated her straight shoulders, attached to a ruffled bodice that made her breasts look full and tempting. The waist was fitted, the skirt slightly flaring. A wide border of Mallorcan needlework in shining threads of gold, blue, and white graced the hemline.

As it happened, Celia's prized sandals went perfectly with Jane's new dress, so they each bought a pair. Or rather, Celia did, handing over Francisco's money with élan as Jane frantically tried to equate dollars and pesetas to discover how much she was spending. Her rough calculations told her that they were in the hundreds-of-dollars range, and Jane was plainly shocked.

Celia laughed as they sat in the shade of a sidewalk café sipping iced coffee. "Don't concern yourself with the money, Señorita Burton. Francisco has plenty of it."

Jane made rings on the wooden table with the bottom of her glass, feeling conspicuous in her new clothes. "I'm not used to letting strangers buy me things, that's all."

Celia leaned back in her chair. "Would you mind very much if I called you Jane?"

Jane shook her head. "On the contrary, I'd prefer it."

"*Bien*. It seems to me that you and Francisco are not quite strangers. Emilio and I both assumed that you were someone very special."

Jane shifted. "Why? Because Francisco's paying for my new outfit?"

Celia's gaze was frankly speculative. Her eyes moved between fringes of heavy black lashes. "What do you know of Francisco? There is much to learn about that man."

Should she admit that she knew about María? Jane sipped her iced coffee. "Not much," she hedged. "We really are little more than strangers." At least in some ways, she amended silently.

"*Bueno*. My Francisco." she chuckled at Jane's surprised expression. "I call him mine because he's like a brother to me. I've known Francisco ever since I was a baby. We grew up in the same *barrio* in Madrid. It was a hideous place, Rats, cockroaches, broken glass, and sickness. His mother was our *medico*, a heaven-sent saint. She had no training, no money for medicines, but she cured our ailments with herbs and common sense. Many owe their lives to her. Now she lives in a lovely villa on the outskirts of the city, and I praise God that she may live out her old age in comfort." Unconsciously she crossed herself.

"But if they were so poor . . ." Jane toyed with a cork coaster.

"Francisco," Celia said proudly. "He worked like a dog to free us from that life! He loaded trucks, he worked in a slaughterhouse, *niña*, he even cleaned sewers to make money! Even though he had to stop going to school, he slaved to send his brothers and sisters and his cousins. And me, although I was no relation. I was his cousin's best friend, and that was reason enough for him. She was his favorite. Her name was María."

Jane swallowed. "I know. She died in a diving accident."

Celia was astonished. "Did Francisco tell you?"

"No. Someone else did," Jane murmured.

"*Ay*, he would be furious if he thought that anyone else knew his secret! He loved María more than anybody except his mother, I think. He used to boast of her school grades, her intelligence and wit, while he stood there covered in blood from the slaughterhouse. He's a remarkable man, *señorita*. The woman who catches him should light a candle every day for the rest to her life!"

"Well, I'm not going to 'catch him,' " Jane said firmly.

"But we thought . . ." Celia gestured with her hands. "You see, Francisco has never taken a woman on his voyages before!"

"He's never had to. I was forced on him." She told Celia the whole story. "So you see," she concluded, "there's nothing special about me." Except that the mere thought of him makes me go weak, she thought. Except that, in his arms, I feel as I have never felt before.

The woman looked unconvinced. "Still, the way he looks at you, the way he touches you . . . there's something there. Oh, I know he's had his share of women—after all, he is a man—but with you, it's more. I can tell."

Jane studied her drink. "No, Celia. You're wrong. I drive him crazy, and vice versa, but it's so different back in the

States, between men and women, I mean.'' She hesitated, not knowing how to explain the difference tactfully.

''In what way?'' Celia hailed the handsome waiter for another round. The man inclined his head politely and disappeared.

''Well, take the issue of working, for example. Francisco thinks women shouldn't have jobs if their husbands can support them! I don't happen to agree.''

Celia smiled knowingly. ''Ah, the liberation of women. That's the problem. I suspected as much, *amiga mia*. It's true that, as a group, Spanish men aren't as progressive in that area as some of your men. But they're years ahead in others.''

Jane frowned. ''Such as?''

The Spanish woman's eyes softened. ''Such as my Emilio. No man treats his wife with more respect and care. A man like that is hard to find. Francisco will be the same, when he marries. Oh, he may make a lot of noises about what his wife will and will not do, but our men don't mean half of it. It's their . . . what do you call it? We say *machismo*.''

''We say the same thing.'' Sighing, Jane took the glass the waiter offered. Her eyes widened when he handed her a single perfect rose. He turned to Celia and spoke in Spanish.

''It's from the café's owner,'' Celia translated. ''He wants to thank you for gracing his table today.''

Jane blushed. ''Oh, come on!''

Celia waved her hand. ''Such are the men of Spain. Do you see what I mean?''

Jane laid the rose down carefully and picked up her iced coffee.

''Sometimes, when I'm doing things for Emilio, such as washing his shirts by hand, or combing his hair, I say to myself, 'Celia, you are crazy to act like this man's slave!' But, Jane, when you really care for someone, you want to be his slave. To please him, to make his life easy and gracious.'' She gestured to the rose. ''That is the Spanish way.'' Celia's eyes narrowed slyly. ''That is Francisco's way, too.''

A slave of love. He had said it himself.

"Well, it's a very interesting philosophy," Jane said vaguely, "but it doesn't really matter. I'll be going back to California at the end of the hunt."

"Would you stay if he asked you to?" Celia pressed.

Jane swallowed. "He's not going to," she said, and she was astonished at the storm of emotions that rose in her at the idea. There were disbelief and fear, but a wild, riotous hope overshadowed everything else. If he asked her to stay! Oh, would he? Was there the slightest possibility?

"Jane," Celia said archly, "you give up nothing when you love a man. You only gain."

"I'm sorry, Celia," she managed, her mind whirling. "But I'm not sure that's true."

Celia grinned. "We shall see."

It was three-fifteen. Celia announced that they'd better head for Café Hortensia, and they window-shopped down several streets. The balmy air was filled with ocean smells, fish and salt and seaweed. Lovely Mallorcan women dressed in the latest fashions strode past, shopping bags on their tanned arms. Tall, dark-haired men ogled them, calling and hooting. As before, Celia took no notice.

"Here we are," she said, opening a leaded-glass door in a Georgian-style building.

The room was done up as an English tearoom, with Victorian chandeliers and bentwood chairs. Red flocked paper covered the walls and women in mob caps and floor-length pinafores over black dresses carried trays of espresso and pastries.

Francisco was sitting in the corner with his back to them. Across from him lounged an elegant woman dressed in a lavender silk dress. She smiled at him indolently as his fingers crept up her arm.

"*Ay*, Francisco," Celia muttered. "He never quits." She headed straight for the table. Jane held back.

Celia chuckled. "Don't think a thing of it, *amiga*. Francisco is always flirting. He doesn't mean anything. If you were Spanish, you'd understand."

Well, she wasn't Spanish. She didn't understand. The magic of last night settled like ashes in her throat.

"Celia!" the elegant woman cried, rising from her chair. They embraced.

Francisco turned, obviously looking for Jane. His eyes brightened when he saw her, and he hurried to her side, kissing her lightly. "Juanita, how beautiful!" he cried. Then he lowered his voice. "How many people would we shock if I threw you to the floor and began to make love to you?"

"Your friend, for one," Jane said unsteadily. His eyes were melting her, his gaze like fire. She licked her lips self-consciously.

"Every inch a beauty," he breathed. Encircling her waist with his hand, he drew her toward the table. "Señora Hortensia Bauza, may I present Señorita Jane Burton of the United States?" he said formally.

Hortensia Bauza touched cheeks with Jane and asked her to sit down. "We're drinking *palo*," she said. "Would you care for a glass?"

"It's a liqueur," Francisco explained. "I think you'd like it."

"Just some tea for me," Celia said. "*Palo* makes me sleepy."

"I'd like to try the *palo*." Jane shifted in her chair, wishing she hadn't seen Francisco's fingers on Hortensia's arms.

Francisco beamed with approval. Jane gave him a weak smile.

"Well, *señor*, here you are as usual, with a table full of ladies!" Hortensia laughed. "Don't you know any men?"

He shook his head. "Doña Tensia, you'll be giving me a bad reputation.!"

"A prize you richly deserve," she retorted, gesturing a waitress over. "Señorita Burton, Don Francisco tells me you wish to call the United States. My husband is arranging the call through his office. We should hurry with our drinks and go.''

''That's very kind of you,'' Jane murmured. So she was married. Somehow, that dulled the edges of Jane's jealousy.

Jealous? I am not jealous! she told herself. I have no hold on Francisco.

Which is just the problem, a hateful little voice inside her taunted.

Their drinks came, and Jane downed hers quickly, to the amusement of Francisco and Hortensia, who sipped theirs like two pampered Siamese cats presented with yet another pail of cream.

When they finally finished, the group left to make the call. Hortensia's husband, an importer, kept his office next door. It was filled with half-opened crates. ''Samples,'' Señor Bauza explained, as he left Francisco and Jane alone with the telephone. It was already ringing.

''Don't forget that it's only eight in the morning there,'' Francisco told her.

''Chuck's a night person,'' she said, knowing he wouldn't understand her wry joke.

The phone rang and rang.

Jane slumped and set the phone in the cradle. ''I guess he's out,'' she said. Maybe already on his way to the school, she considered doubtfully. Oh, what was happening to the school? Would there still be one when she returned?

Francisco touched her cheek. ''Don't worry, *querida*. We'll call again tomorrow. All right?''

She managed a smile for him. ''All right. Thank you.''

''I want you happy,'' he replied, moving aside a box of plastic coasters embossed with palm trees and the words ''Palma de Mallorca.'' He kissed her, then held her tightly. ''He'll be there when we call next time.''

They found Celia and Hortensia in the outer office, chatting while Celia leafed through the Spanish edition of *Vogue*. They smiled at Jane and Francisco.

"How is your uncle, Señorita Burton?" Hortensia asked.

"He wasn't home," Francisco told her. "May we come back tomorrow morning and try again?"

"But of course," the woman said graciously. "As we say in Spain, 'My telephone is your telephone.' May I invite you back to the café?"

"Tensia, Celia, would you mind very much if Jane and I abandoned the two of you? We have a few more errands."

The women shrugged. "Of course not, Francisco!" Hortensia said.

"I have to retrieve Emi at the boat anyway, no?" Celia put the magazine down and rose.

He nodded. "He should be finished by now. I know this is unforgivable, but I . . ." He trailed off.

Celia's smile was sly and knowing. She shared it with Señora Bauza. "You don't need to make excuses to us, *amigo*. Emi and I will meet you at La Bodega, *sí*? In an hour?"

"Won't you and Jaime join us for dinner and flamenco?" Francisco asked Hortensia.

She shook her head. "Unfortunately, we already have plans. I'm sorry I can't hear more about your treasure hunt. And about America, *señorita*."

"Perhaps tomorrow," Francisco replied. "Celia, until later . . ."

Francisco led Jane through a maze of streets and squares, going from brilliant sunlight to cool shade, and back again. This time she noticed, there were no insulting catcalls and hoots. It was as if she were invisible beside Francisco.

At last they came to a tiny whitewashed building, its small cross-topped dome glinting in the sunlight. Together they climbed the limestone steps. Then Francisco paused before the arched wooden doors.

"Have you a scarf?" he asked her. "This is a Catholic church."

"Yes, somewhere." She dug in her purse. "It's sort of wrinkled, though." Sheepishly she unwadded an old piece of red chiffon and showed it to him.

"It's fine." He waited while she draped it over her head.

"Do you mind this very much?" he asked. "I thought it might soothe you. I usually come here when I'm in port. It's a good place to think."

He could be so kind, she thought. Smiling, she squeezed his hand. "Thank you."

They climbed the stairs. "Is this where the crew came for Mass?"

"*Sí.* It's dedicated to sailors." He ushered her in.

She caught her breath. The interior was splashed with golden sunbeams which streamed in through an overhead skylight. A crucifix made of a thousand tiny shells hung on a bare white wall before a plain altar of olive wood. On either side, rows of votive candles in red glasses flickered and sputtered, casting shadows on a painted statue of the Virgin Mary. Her arms were outstretched as if to embrace all the troubled souls who prayed to her for intervention. Fresh flowers of pink and lavender lay at her feet. The dome was painted with a mural of Jesus walking on the water, while the Apostles called to him from a storm-tossed boat. A sailor's comfort, indeed.

Shutting the door, Francisco dipped his finger in a small font of holy water and crossed himself. Then he genuflected before the cross and slipped into the last pew.

Jane sat beside him, as a sense of peace stole over her. There was something very intimate in his sharing this with her.

The rays of light from the ceiling shifted slowly, and finally Francisco sighed. Crossing himself, he rose to his feet. Then he grasped her elbow and moved her to the aisle. Together they walked toward the altar.

Like a bride and groom, she found herself thinking. Coloring, she tried to push the image out of her mind. But it wouldn't go. She pictured herself in white, coming down the aisle on Uncle Chuck's arm, carrying a bouquet of white roses and baby's breath. . . .

He put some money in a wooden box and handed her a candle. "Make a wish," he whispered. "Say a prayer."

With her lips, she prayed that they would find *El Corazón*. But with her heart she prayed that he would ask her to stay, to be his *mujer*, to be his . . . She was afraid to say the word.

They stood together before the simple cross in the simple church. Then silently Francisco led her outside to the bustle of Palma and their rendezvous with the Olivetas.

But a little part of her remained within the walls of the Church of San Pedro.

Chapter Six

La Bodega was hot and smoky. Jane, Francisco, Emilio, and Celia sat in bentwood chairs around a round wooden table covered with the clutter of their dinner. Francisco looked happy and relaxed as he chatted with his friends. Jane was proud to sit beside him, feeling pretty in her new clothes. Since their time together at the church, there was a new intimacy between them. As if he could read her thoughts, he smiled at her and touched her dress. "It's lovely," he whispered. "I can't wait to take it off you."

On the stage, the flamenco group returned from their break. The dancer rose from her chair and began to move. The crowd hushed, all eyes on the stage and the figure who dominated it.

Two hands made slow, stiff circles in the dusky light, the fingers extended. Beneath them, the woman's forehead was creased with concentration. Her jet-black hair was parted in the middle and braided at the nape, exposing warm olive shoulders and a back of firm muscles as the woman pivoted in a circle. Her chin jutted forward as her arms traveled in front of her form-fitting black-and-red gown. Below her thighs, the skirt ruffled into a long train, which she now raised in her fist like a Gypsy queen wielding a knife at an enemy. Her heels stamped the floor with severe staccato beats.

"*Ay, mucho,*" Francisco murmured, taut, caught up in the mystery of the flamenco. His voice was low, almost sexual, but it was not erotic tension that filled the room. It was like the force emanating from the consummation of a pagan ritual, one that gripped everyone in the room. The crowd held its collective breath. No one stirred as the woman swayed on the stage, strutting regally, a queen of fire and ice.

"*Mucho,*" Emilio echoed. He clapped his hands together once, very softly.

Then the guitar struck into the hushed twilight. The singer began a wild Gypsy wail, unnerving Jane with its mysterious intensity. There is something here, she thought, something I don't understand but I want to. I want to be a part of it; I want to feel what Francisco is feeling.

She studied him. He leaned forward in his chair, his back as stiff as the dancer's, barely breathing, part of the ceremony.

The dancer burst into a frenzy of heel stamps and quick turns. She was a blur as she threw herself into the rite, a black-and-red explosion of fervor and implacable passion. Francisco inhaled sharply between his teeth and bit his lower lip.

Faster and faster she danced, a whirl of drama and emotion. The singer clapped her hands in a strange, arhythmic pattern. The guitarist sat hunched over his strings. Jane thought of the music on the beach, of the passion that had erupted inside her. It was happening again.

"*Mucho,*" Francisco whispered. "*Ay, brava!*"

The dance crescendoed into a climax that transported the dancer past movement, past emotion. She raised her face to the spotlight that bathed her face with white, clenching her teeth. She stamped with all her might, fulfilling the music, fulfilling her reason for being.

Then it was over. Panting, perspiration dragging her makeup down her face, the woman froze. "*Olé!*" the cry went up. "*Olé!*"

She bowed and took her chair beside the guitarist, seemingly exhausted. Yet he began to play once more, and when the music urged her to it, she sprang from her chair and danced again. On and on the music played, transporting the audience. Then finally she finished in a blaze of passion, nearly collapsing on the stage. The cries of "*Olé!*" were loud and impassioned.

Francisco sipped his *manzanilla,* a dry Spanish sherry, and leaned back his head. "I'm exhausted," he groaned.

Emilio laughed. "*Magnífico,* no? Didn't I tell you this was the best flamenco bar in town?"

Francisco touched Jane's hand. "And you? How did you like it?"

She was at a loss to describe to him the effect the dance had had on her, though she had no trouble explaining it to herself. It was the same exhilaration, the same yearning she felt when beneath the sea. That, too, was a form of worship so fervent, so complete that it made her feel primitive.

"Incredible," she said at last, but the word didn't do justice to what she had seen, and she knew it.

But Francisco smiled with delight. His white teeth flashed in the sultry room. "I'm so pleased you liked it." Taking in her new clothes with a satisfied gaze, he winked at Celia. "Blue was the right color, *sí*? She's bewitching."

"I couldn't agree more," Emilio drawled. Celia made a great show of punching him on the arm.

"I hate to break up the party," Francisco said, stroking Jane's fingertips, "but Jane and I have to get up in a few hours. It's almost two."

He stood and pulled Jane's chair out for her. Then he led the way to the hat-check area to retrieve the shawl that Celia had lent her.

"Jane and I need to comb our hair," Celia announced, pulling her with her. "*Verdad, amiga*?"

"Oh, yes," Jane blurted, flushing as the two men regarded them humorously. "We'll be right back."

They went inside the enormous ladies' room, decked out in garish hand-painted tiles and gilt-framed mirrors.

Celia leaned against a wall and crossed her arms. "Well?"

"Well, what?" Jane mimicked Celia's stance.

"He's in love with you, *idiota*. He doesn't know it yet. But by the end of the treasure hunt, he will beg you to become la Señora Juana Burton de Pontalba!"

Jane's heart leaped. Just as quickly, she shook her head at her impulsive new friend. "Don't be silly. And my name is Jane. Plain old Jane."

"Not plain. Not old. Just the woman for my Francisco. Oh, I almost forgot." Celia dug around in her purse and held up a pearl earring. "Did you leave this in the car today? I found it on the backseat."

Jane shook her head. "No. It's for pierced ears, see? I don't have . . ." She stopped speaking.

Celia's face had drained of its lovely color. She took a slow, deep breath.

"Are you all right?" Jane asked. "Did I say something?"

A strange smile passed across the Spanish woman's features. It was infinitely wise and sad, pained and amused. "No," she said, depositing the earring back in her purse. "Come, the men are waiting."

They saw Francisco leaning over the counter, murmuring to the hat-check girl, whose face was a wreath of rosy blushes.

"Ahem." Celia put her hands on her hips. "We're back."

"*Ay*, caught!" Francisco laughed easily, draping the white shawl around Jane's bare shoulders with infinite care. The hat-check girl gave him a pert smile and disappeared.

"Francisco, you're such a flirt," Celia accused. There was a faint tremor in her voice. Francisco eyed her. The silent messages of two old friends passed between them. Then Celia moved past him and took Emilio's hand.

The four of them walked to the Mercedes. Celia and Jane sat in the backseat together, and Francisco and Emilio chatted in rapid Spanish in the front.

Jane glanced out the window as they sped back to the boat. There was phosphorescence in the sea tonight, caused by thousands and thousands of tiny plankton which glowed when they moved, turning the waves an undulating shimmering, vivid green. She turned to point it out to Celia, just in time to see her take the pearl earring out of her purse and lay it carefully on the upholstery.

They reached the cove where the boat was docked. Emilio pulled the Mercedes over and the four of them got out. They stood in a group at the edge of the cliff. The phosphorescence cast shimmering lime shadows on the sand. Bathed in the soft glow, the crew sprawled in their bedrolls in the encampment.

"Francisco's babies," Celia teased. "Imagine, they went to Mass today while you drank and swore!"

Francisco tousled her hair. "You always were a little brat," he said fondly. "Emilio, how do you keep her in line?"

Emilio planted a wet buss on Celia's cheek. "I'll tell you all about it one day, *amigo*." He gestured to the *Fortuna*, bobbing in the water. "I'll do a last check on everything tomorrow. You're taking Jane back to Jaime Bauza's for another phone call, *sí*?"

Francisco nodded. "*Gracias, hombre*."

Emilio laughed. "Don't thank me! You pay me well. *Buenas noches*." He embraced Francisco and patted Jane's hand. "*Ay*, for a good-night kiss from you, *maja*!"

Jane thought of the earring. He's having an affair, she thought miserably. And Celia knows it. She remembered how Celia's eyes had shone with love when she had talked about her husband that afternoon. "You want to be his slave," Celia had declared, while her husband was with another woman. The situation tore at Jane's heart; in spite of the short time she had known Celia, she cared for her very much.

Celia laughed gaily. "You'd better watch it, *querido*. Francisco is the jealous type!"

"To my regret." Emilio sighed. "Francisco, don't let this one get away. She's an angel."

"Emi, you're embarrassing Jane," Celia admonished.

"What about me?" Francisco drawled.

"It's impossible to embarrass you," Celia shot back. "You have no shame!"

Francisco made a great show of being hurt.

Celia rolled her eyes. "Men! They're impossible! Why do we put up with them, Juanita?"

Emilio threw his arm around his wife. "Because you can't live without us! We're . . . what is the word I want? Francisco, help me! We are . . ."

"Male chauvinist pigs," Francisco whispered to Jane. "Isn't that so, *mi amor*?"

"More than you know," she said grimly.

Celia touched Jane's hand. "It was so wonderful to meet you, *amiga*." They traded glances. Oh, God, she's forgiven him, Jane thought. He's cheating on her, and she loves him anyway!

"*Bueno*, now it's almost three," Francisco cut in. "We've got to get some sleep!"

Emilio opened his mouth as if to say something, but he closed it and nodded. "You're right, *compadre*. It was my pleasure to meet you, *señorita*. I hope you find what you're looking for." He winked, and Jane colored.

"Thank you. And thank you, Celia, for everything. I had a wonderful time."

The two women hugged each other. "It's all right," Celia whispered. "I meant what I said about Emi." She slid her hand around her husband's waist. "Come on, *papacito*, let's go home."

"*Ay*, when you use that tone . . ." He grinned at Francisco. "You may get some sleep, but I doubt if I will!"

"*Adiós*."

"*Buenas noches*."

Francisco and Jane waved to the Olivetas as the Mercedes faded down the highway. Then Francisco pulled her into his arms and held her without speaking. The moon glowed on his hair, shading his face as he sighed. Pressing her close, he breathed deeply, as if inhaling her perfume.

Jane did the same, matching his slow, deep rhythm. Their chests rose and fell in unison, in, out. A calming peace stole over her, and she leaned against him languidly. Inhale, exhale. She let go of her sadness for Celia. Her friend wouldn't want her to grieve for her.

Francisco's heart beat steadily against her ear. His skin was so warm, lightly scented with sandalwood and the heady aromas of the Mallorcan night. She nuzzled against the coarse hairs of his chest, feeling his medallion graze her forehead as he bent to press his chin against the crown of her head.

His hands flattened against her back and he sighed again, a faint smile on his lips. His long lashes brushed his cheeks as he closed his eyes and felt her breathing against him. It was like the first time, when he had pushed his air into her lungs. The other-worldly quality of their lovemaking had overwhelmed her then; thinking of it now, she was stirred by the sensations. She circled him with her arms, her fingers pressed into the muscles of his back, and held him.

They tightened around each other, immersed in the awakening force of their need. Jane felt it in him as surely as she felt it in herself. It was as if she could read his soul—not his mind, not his body, but the vital thing that was Francisco and which wanted her tonight more than anything else in the universe. It made her feel power and joy and completion. It made her feel like a princess.

He must have sensed her feelings. "It is like the dance," he murmured. "The flamenco." Wordlessly she agreed. It was the essence of passion, this stillness, this fierce concentration. It was the most erotic thing she had ever experienced.

He touched her hair, a caress that began at the crown of her head and ended with the curled ends of honey brown. Bringing the strands to his lips, he kissed them reverently. Jane closed her eyes as she felt his desire grow. Soon the stillness would end and they would explode into a thousand stars screaming across the night. Soon she would die in his arms, only to live again, reborn in the ecstasy he created for her.

His hands rounded her shoulders, his fingers massaging the hollows beneath her collarbones. "*Dios*, I wish I had a bed to put you in," he breathed, his body responding to her nearness. "A bed covered with satin the color of your eyes. I would put roses in your hair, and I would come to you like a king. I would make love to you until the sun rose."

His nails ran along the top of her dress, outlining the rising swell of her breasts. Moaning deep in his throat, he unfastened the silken cords and peeled the dress away, exposing her breasts. "Petals of my rose," he whispered. "My sweet flower, come to my garden."

Before she could answer, Francisco covered her mouth with his, a kiss so tender, so gentle that it brought tears to her eyes. He barely touched her at first, his breath a light caress as he closed his eyes in concentration. His lips were soft as he parted them, inching over hers in a series of slow, restrained kisses. Taking her lower lip between his teeth, he nipped ever so carefully, with such devotion, that Jane could do nothing but surrender to the delight he gave her.

His fingers found her nipples and he touched them with feathery motions. Jane trembled in his arms.

"You're with me." His hushed voice was filled with triumph. "You want me."

In reply, she squeezed his hand over her breast. Light flared in his eyes, and his chest heaved with emotion.

"*Olé*," he whispered. *Olé*, my queen."

He bent her back in his arms, crushing his body against her arched chest, bruising her with white-hot kisses from her forehead to her navel, yanking down her dress with impatient, shaking fingers. She threw her arms around his neck and he reached beneath her dress, yanking at her panties, pushing the skirt above her hips to expose the soft, secret place that begged for him in a rush of desire. She was drowning with it, inflamed, ready.

"No. Not here." Taking a deep breath, he smoothed her dress and held her flushed face between his hands. "We'll go

to the boat. I have at least a small bed to give you." He knelt
in the sand, unfastening her new shoes and sliding them off
her feet.

They tiptoed past the sleeping men, sprawled on the sand
beside the dead campfire. Ricardo snored like a trumpet.

Francisco took off his shoes and waded into the magical,
glowing water. With each movement, the sea gave off green
sparks, so eerily beautiful that Jane thought of the fairy-tale
books of her childhood.

Then he helped her into the boat and shoved off, jumping
in with graceful, controlled movements. The oars dipped into
the bewitched waters, lighting up the sea in rings around the
dinghy.

"I could take you now," he murmured. "I can hardly
stand to wait." He let go of the oar to touch her thigh,
pushing up her dress. "Mine. Tonight, Jane, you belong to
me."

And you? Do you belong to me? she wanted to ask. But
she was afraid to, fearful that the answer might be no.

And why should that matter? They had no ties. This was
only for the summer, no matter what Celia prophesied. Anything else was ridiculous. There was no future for them. . . .

"Why do you look so sad, *mi amor?*" Francisco whispered.
He looked troubled.

"Do I?" she asked, startled. "I'm not. Really. I'm very
happy."

"Jane." He said her name as if it were a prayer. "Jane, I
want this night to last forever. Before God, I swear I will
please you tonight."

They reached the *Fortuna* with no further words between
them. Above them, the stars filled the sky, sending their
points of light into Francisco's eyes. He helped her onto the
deck, sliding her body against his, and kissed her once, his
fingers seeking out the sensitive flesh around her ears. Then,
hand in hand, they headed for the ladder that would take them
to his cabin.

* * *

He lit a hurricane lamp, his shadow growing as he adjusted the flame. The boat rocked with the calm waves, the glowing green water slapping against the wood, a sound as old as the sea itself. It mingled with the gurgle of crimson wine as Francisco poured it into a glass.

He drank, then handed the glass to Jane. It was a pleasing gesture, one that spoke of their intimacy. Smiling, Jane accepted the cup.

Francisco lay beside her on the bed, propped on his elbows as he savored the dry burgundy. He leaned back his head, his profile showing in bas-relief against the flickering light, sharp, angular, proud. The medallion gleamed against his bronze skin.

"Is that a religious medal?" Jane asked. He touched it as if he were surprised to find it around his neck.

"No," he said. "An old man gave it to me. He found it in Vigo bay. He was on the expedition with Cousteau. Do you know of that adventure?"

She shook her head. His expression became dreamy and distant.

"An armada of seventeen galleons went down in 1702. They were loaded with precious stones, gold, and silver. My old friend was on one of the many expeditions that have searched for them. They found a few things, but not the main haul."

He touched the medallion again. "Those ships must have been magnificent."

Like you, Jane thought. You are magnificent. He was the last of his kind—a bold adventurer, a corsair thrust into the twentieth century by a quirk of fate, a romantic born into an unromantic world.

And I? she wondered. What am I, that I'm so captivated by him? What causes this instinctive attraction to him?

Attraction? Call it by its proper name. Call it . . .

"Jane." Francisco set down the wine and rolled over on

his stomach. He stroked her face like a cat, pulling her down beside him. The oil lamp sputtered in the breeze from the porthole, shifting the shadows on her body as he undressed her. He slid her dress away, studying her breasts, the flatness of her stomach, the gentle curve of her hips. Then he peeled off her half-slip and her panties. He sipped his wine, surveying her nude form with a proprietary air as she lay quietly beside him.

He brought the glass to her lips. The wine was sweet, but not so sweet as the kiss that followed.

"You are so exquisite," he gasped, caressing her breasts, then sweeping down to gather her buttocks in his palms. "So firm, so soft. A thousand men must want you. And I alone shall have you."

"Yes." It was a plea. Take me with you, to your fierce pirate world, she thought. Take me where men like you exist, where they make women believe in the old ways again. Take me.

"You are the elements. Fire and water. How can one woman be so much?"

"Francisco," she said. "Francisco . . ." The very sound of his name made her quiver with eagerness. She clutched at his shirt, unbuttoning it. He allowed it, holding himself still. His tiny male nipples were erect; she pressed her lips against one of them and thrilled at the gasp of pleasure that shuddered through him.

Hurrying now, she yanked the shirt off, burying her face in his chest. He moved his neck in a slow circle, a low, guttural moan vibrating in his rib cage.

She found his belt and unhooked it. Francisco caught his breath as she unzipped his pants. "So wanton," he purred. "A lady wouldn't dare . . ."

He stood and stepped out of his clothes, standing naked before her. Jane lay back against the rumpled sheet and held out her arms.

"My rose," he breathed. "My rose of the sea." Poising

himself above her, he ordered, "Open yourself for me, Juanita. Give yourself to me."

She obeyed. With a cry, Francisco plunged inside her. Jane arched tautly, unprepared for the savagery of his assault, but welcoming it. They gripped each other, their coupling fierce, frenzied, and abandoned. Gone were the tenderness, the lassitude. Now they writhed and struggled toward the culmination of the dance, faster, harder, stronger, deeper. Tears streamed down Jane's cheeks, wetting Francisco's jaw as he buried his face in her hair. She thrashed like a wild thing; he caught her and seized her, taking her, riding her, mastering her.

Then she stiffened, throwing her head back as her body raised off the bed. A groan escaped her as a violent tremor roared through every fiber of her being. She exploded into a thousand beams of light, the pure energy of rapture. Far away, Francisco echoed her cry and joined her, somewhere in the dazzling heavens, past pleasure, past ecstasy.

The boat creaked rhythmically as at last they lay still, bathed in a sheen of perspiration.

Francisco peered up at her and touched her cheek. "Tears, *mi amor*? Have I moved you so?"

Shyly she nodded.

He smiled at her. "I'm glad." He rolled away and took a drink of wine. Then he brushed her hair away from her face and studied it. "You haven't been with many men, have you?" It wasn't really a question.

She quailed. Did it show somehow? Was she awkward?

"Have you been with many women?" she countered.

He raised his brows. "But of course," he said gently. "I am a man."

"Oh." Why had she asked? She already knew that that was what he would say. After all, she had seen it with her own eyes—in port only one day, and he had flirted outrageously with every lovely woman he saw!

There was a strained silence between them. Finally Francisco kissed her shoulder and rubbed his cheek along her arm. "Did you have a nice day with Celia? You two certainly seemed like old *comadres*!"

"I liked Celia a lot," she told him, warming to him again. "I haven't had many girlfriends. I was such a tomboy when I was small! Back home, I'm too busy."

A ghost of a frown clouded his face. "That's typically American. In Spain, we're never too busy for friends. And a woman should have girlfriends. Men don't know how to be friends with women. They're always thinking of them in sexual terms."

Jane cocked her head. "Always? What about you and Celia?"

He was plainly shocked. "Jane, Celia is a sister to me! I would never—"

"You're friends, then," she pointed out.

He sighed. "There's a fault in your logic. I don't know what it is, but I know you're wrong, *maja*."

"What does that mean?" she asked, switching the subject. It seemed that everywhere they trod, they found thin ice. The cultural barrier was becoming a gap that might never be closed. "Everyone's always calling me *maja*!"

His head jerked up. "Who? Who calls you that?"

Startled, she looked at him. His face was rigid with displeasure, the muscles in his jaw working. Her fierce corsair.

"I don't know," she said vaguely. "I just hear it now and then. Why? Is it something dirty?"

His face blanked for a moment. Then he smiled. "No. It means 'beautiful' or 'sexy.' It's slang. As you might call someone a fox." He stroked her forehead and sipped his burgundy. "But in Spain, strange men don't call a woman *maja*. It shows disrespect."

But they trail their fingers along their arms, she thought, lowering her gaze. They murmur to them while their wives and dates are out of sight. A great sadness washed over her.

Did Francisco have any idea how many of her waking hours she spent thinking of him?

He moved, making her aware of his nude body, of the long, limber muscles of his legs as they hung over the bed. Of so much else. . . .

"Spanish men must love their women differently than your American men," he mused. "I can't believe Americans know how to do it properly."

Jane began to smile. "That's your machismo showing," she teased. But he hadn't heard her.

"What do your Americans know of love?" he went on. "They're too busy watching football games and polishing their sports cars! They act as if they believe in women's liberation, but they seize it as an excuse to neglect you."

Jane's lips parted. "Neglect? How?"

"We Spanish men, we treat our women like flowers— fragile, precious. They need to be handled with much love and care. They need the sunlight and the rain, the happy times and the sad. And they need us. Without us, without our adoration and attention, they wither."

"And if they wither?" she asked softly, thinking of Celia. "If you don't take proper care of them?"

He paused. "We weep," he whispered. "Jane, we weep."

A haunted, hollow look crept into his eyes. He's thinking of María, she realized. His proud shoulders slumped as he lowered his gaze to his hands, as if they were the things that had caused María's death.

Suddenly Jane felt confined in the cabin. It was too small, too warm. There was too much awkwardness between them as they tried to learn about each other. And she didn't want it to be awkward. She wanted it to be as their lovemaking had been—perfect.

Jumping up, she took the wine out of his hand and chucked him under the chin. "Come on! I'll race you!" she cried, streaking out of the cabin. "Come on, lazybones!"

"What?" She heard him run after her as she scurried up the ladder. "Jane, are you crazy?"

She leaped onto the main deck, giggling as he got caught up in the game. He took the rungs two at a time, nearly succeeding in grabbing her foot as she darted away.

"You can't catch me!" she challenged, pleased with herself for distracting him from his sad memories, and herself from the equally poignant reality of their relationship.

He loped after her, jumping over the coiled ropes. "Don't run by the compressors!" he warned. "I'll throw you overboard if you damage anything!"

She climbed over the railing. "Too late!" she cried, and plunged into the water.

The glittering green flashed around her as she swam with all her might. A second later, Francisco joined her in a flood of electric emerald. She dodged his outstretched hands, delighting in the silkiness of the mild water against her naked flesh. Diving under him, she grabbed his foot and tickled the bottom. Francisco jerked convulsively. Freeing himself, he whipped around and caught her by the waist.

"Now I have you!" he cried, laughing like a little boy. "Now I have you!"

"No, you don't!" Squealing, she thrashed out of his grasp and disappeared beneath the surface.

He recaptured her with ease. "*Sí*, I have you!" he exulted.

Jane wrapped herself around him. "Then take me," she cooed.

He arched back in the water, dunking his head so that his hair washed away from his face.

"You are so aggressive," he chided, moving his hands down her sides.

"I know. And you love it."

"Juanita! I do not!"

She tapped her finger against his lips. "Jane, Francis. Just Jane."

They made love, slow underwater love, once again sharing

breath, shimmering like two alien creatures in a vortex of electrified energy. Then Francisco put her on his back and swam through the water, treating her to a ride. They dived beneath the water, breaching the surface, gliding through the magic green like dolphins.

"It's almost dawn," she murmured. "Francisco, we've stayed up· all night!"

"A pity," he replied, smiling. Then he carried her back to the boat, and to his bed.

In the morning, Emilio lent them the Mercedes to drive into Palma. Señor Bauza left them in his office to make the call to California.

It was one in the morning in California. Jane prayed that Chuck and Alejandro would be in, but she had her doubts. In the old days, he'd still be in the bars then.

But someone picked the phone up b; the third ring.

"Hello?" Jane said, surprised.

"Yes?"

"Uncle Chuck? It's Janey!" Francisco grinned at her nickname. Perching on the edge of the desk, he picked up a box of flamenco dolls and peeked under the skirt of one.

"Janey! How are you, honey? Hey, Alex!" he bellowed. "It's Jane!"

"You weren't home when I called before. I'm glad you're home now," she said.

"We just got back from a meeting with our lawyer. Took the old geezer to Mr. A's. What do you think about that? Alex had to tell me which fork to use for what, but I'm getting the hang of it pretty good. Not bad for an old ex-Navy chief, huh?"

"That . . . that's wonderful," she said, astounded. Mr. A's was *the* place to go in San Diego. Men had to wear jackets and ties to be admitted. As far as she knew, the only jacket Chuck owned was the one he'd worn in the Navy—a raggedy old pea coat.

"But why were you out with a lawyer? Is there trouble?" Her heart contracted. She knew she couldn't trust him to run things!

Francisco frowned. He gestured to indicate that he was leaving the room to give her some privacy. She shook her head, but he walked out and shut the door.

"Trouble, hell! Alex and me are going to be partners! We're drawing up the papers and everything. He's paid off all our debts, honey! We're really cooking back here in the old U.S. of A! We've been opening the school up an hour earlier. We're running a class for businessmen who don't want to come in after work. Boosted the month's total by over sixty percent!"

She gaped at the receiver. Was she hearing properly?

"Things are going great! We hired a bookkeeper, too! 'Course, we got an accountant for the big stuff. Anyways, she said you'd done a great job. She also suggested we put in some clothes. You know, those designer trunks and stuff. They're selling great! What? Oh, here, Alex wants to talk to you. I guess this must be costing a lot."

"Señorita Burton? I'm so pleased to hear your voice," Alejandro said graciously. "Dare I hope that you're calling to tell us you've found something?"

"Not yet," she said. "Mr. de Anza, thank you for being so kind to my uncle."

Alejandro laughed. "Chuck is my *compadre*. And I'm not being kind. You have built quite a business here. I'm having the time of my life working with it! I hope you approve of our partnership!"

"Oh, of course," she assured him. "I think it's wonderful."

"*Bueno*. To be honest, I was afraid there might be some hurt feelings on your part. Please don't think for a moment that I'm trying to push you out. But you're more valuable to the school teaching than maintaining the ledgers, no?"

"You're right," she said, but she couldn't help a twinge of jealousy. She'd come to look on the Burton School of Diving as her own. It wouldn't be easy to give up control. As it hadn't been easy on the hunt to acquiesce to Francisco. . . .

"Now, down to the other matter at hand. How do you think progress is going? Is Capitan Pontalba spending my money wisely?"

"Oh, yes. He's working very hard."

"Please keep a good eye on him. Is he being kind to you? I would be very angry with him if I heard otherwise. He isn't giving you a hard time, is he?"

She laughed nervously. If only he knew! "Oh, no! We're getting along very well."

There was a pause. "There's something wrong. I can hear it in your voice."

"Everything's fine."

"Isn't the diving wonderful?" he asked, changing the subject. "*Hostia*, I miss it!"

"Well, I've only gone down once," she said. "But it was very nice. Oh, here's Francisco." She practically flung the receiver at him as he walked back into the room.

"*Bueno*, Alejandro?" Francisco spoke in Spanish. He frowned and eyed Jane. "*Pues, no*," he grumbled. "*No!*" He talked for a long time, tiredly, as if he were on the phone with a small child.

Finally he looked up. His brow was creased and his lips were pursed as he glared at Jane. "Do you wish to say good-bye to your uncle?" His voice was leaden.

Eyes wide, Jane nodded.

"I guess they just had a big fight about the time limit, honey. That guy's been giving you a lot of grief, huh?"

"No. Really, there's no—"

"What's that? Oh, Alex says he's taken care of it. Don't you worry. If you have any more trouble, you just call us and we'll read him the riot act! Here's the old man again."

"Señorita Burton? He is to let you go down! Don't you permit him to abuse you!"

"But—"

"I'm very sorry I have put you through all this. But I appreciate your protecting my interests. I see I need a confederate aboard *La Fortuna*. Pontalba is not the man I thought he was. Again, my apologies. I'll try to make it up to you when you come home. *Adiós.*"

Alejandro broke the connection. Puzzled, Jane set the receiver down and walked to Francisco's side. He was staring out the window.

"Francisco? What's going on?" she asked, touching his shoulder. "What on earth is wrong with Mr. de Anza?"

He whipped around to face her, his expression cool and impassive. "Well, aren't you the clever one," he said, his voice dripping with sarcasm. "*Mr.* de Anza is convinced that I'm beating you daily in hopes that you'll go home—and leave me to keep more than my share of the treasure. He's threatened to pull my financing if I don't 'reform.'"

"I didn't say anything against you," she protested. "I told him the hunt was going very well!"

"So well that he's reducing his support?" His fingers wrapped around the pull cord to the venetian blinds. His knuckles were white.

"What are you talking about?"

"I have two months." He dropped the cord and stuffed his hands into his pockets. "If I don't find *El Corazón* by that time, I'll be forced to call off the expedition."

"No!"

"Oh, yes. But what do you care? You have the money for your school now. Alejandro's going into business with your oh-so-incompetent uncle! You should be happy that he's cutting me off! He'll have more money to spend on you!"

"Francisco, I didn't say anything!" she cried. She grabbed his wrist. "You must believe me!"

"Alejandro said a great many things to me," he replied, staring at her fingers. "There's nowhere else he could have heard them than from your lips."

He shook her off. She gasped as if he had physically hurt her. "Let's go. We have to cast off as soon as possible. But let me tell you, *señorita*, if it were up to me, you'd be on your way to the airport right now."

Chapter Seven

In the morning, they sped into the open sea. A school of dolphins frolicked around them, as if leading the way to *El Corazón*. The sky above was clear and blue, reflecting in the still Mediterranean as the *Fortuna* cut through it. Seabirds squawked overhead, seeking the source of the smells that wafted from the galley.

But it was impossible for Jane to enjoy the beautiful, living seascape around her. Her eyes ached with unshed tears and she had a headache. Francisco hadn't spoken another word to her since their conversation in Señor Bauza's office. He'd canceled their date with Emilio and Celia, whisking her onto the boat without giving her a chance to even say good-bye to them.

What was worse, the little acceptance the crew had favored her with completely evaporated. They avoided her carefully, not even acknowledging her presence unless it was absolutely necessary. The air around Don Francisco was chill and filled with thunderclouds whenever he got near her, and the others took note of it. Only Ricardo dared to talk to the American lady, who for some reason had fallen out of favor with *el jefe*.

The more she thought about what was happening between them, the more furious Jane became. She didn't know what Alejandro had said to him, but it wasn't fair of Francisco to blame her for it without at least listening to her. She had said nothing, nothing! In fact, she'd gone out of her way not to mention anything that would make him look bad. And there were a few things she could have told Alejandro . . .

She leaned her head against the cold metal of the air compressor. From her vantage point she could see directly into the navigation cabin. Francisco crouched in front of the magnetometer readout display, calling out measurements to Hans. Hans would change course according to the increase or decrease in the numbers, which reflected the variation in the strength of the magnetic field below the surface. High numbers indicated the presence of metal, and it was high numbers they sought. That meant ship fittings and cannon. That meant gold and jewels and priceless antiquities.

But they found nothing. The numbers remained low as the hours passed by. The sun reached its zenith and arched low in the sky, and still nothing. At his post in the stern, Carlos bowed his head and crossed himself. In the galley, Ricardo hung a wooden rosary beside the bag of onions and murmured a prayer.

The day ebbed into night. Jane kept her distance from Francisco at the *cena*, eating her marinated fish and rice beside Ricardo, as if he were her bodyguard. Even the little cook was quiet, lost in thought about *El Corazón*. There were no guitars tonight, no lively singing and joking.

She was the first to finish. She carried her plate to the galley and rinsed it, then made her way to her cabin.

Taking off her shorts and tank top, she gazed out the porthole and sighed. Last night had been so different, filled with Francisco and Celia's predictions for the future. It felt awful to be alone again—and she would be alone when the hunt was ended. Francisco would stay in his world, and she would return to hers, bitter, sad, hurt.

Folding her arms beneath her head, she replayed the conversation in Señor Bauza's office, as she had a thousand times before. What had she said? She'd given no hint of trouble! Why would she have, when she and Francisco had been getting along so well?

She thought of the Church of San Pedro, and tears sprang to her eyes. What a fool she had been, to think he had ever felt the closeness she had. The caring . . .

Go ahead, you idiot, she chided. Call it by its proper name. Call it love. You've gone and fallen in love with a man who thinks you're manipulative and devious and all the other things women are supposed to be! You're the romantic, not he! Imagining all sorts of things where nothing existed!

But that's what he was doing—imagining that she had spoken against him. Thanks to Alejandro, who either had misunderstood by accident or on purpose. But why?

Perhaps he had tired of the hunt and needed an excuse to get out of it. But that didn't seem to fit, when he and Chuck had spent so much of their youth searching for treasure. Maybe he'd decided it was too risky, and he saw the diving school as a surer way to increase his fortunes. But he'd dreamed of finding treasure, not business profits! Did people's dreams fade with age?

Francisco's wouldn't. She knew that as surely as she knew that he was being unfair to her. Unbidden, an image of him rose in mind: lying naked beside her in the moonlight, sipping his burgundy, and telling her about his medallion. How close they'd seemed that night!

But that must have been a silly dream, too. No man who felt a bond with a woman would jump to the conclusions that he had. Of course, there was always the possibility that Alejandro was right to worry about Francisco. Maybe he wasn't a good treasure hunter. Maybe Alejandro had heard something that indicated that Francisco was untrustworthy, that he actually was planning to keep more than his share of the find.

But that was impossible. She knew Francisco too well.

"Oh, do you?" she asked herself aloud. "Do you know him at all? You don't even know if he cared for you while you were throwing yourself into his bed! A promiscuous American, that's you, Jane Marie!"

There were footsteps in the hall. Jane stiffened on the bed, listening. They came down the corridor, toward Francisco's cabin. Then they turned toward her quarters. She caught her breath, her heart thudding.

He was standing in front of her door. She could almost hear his hesitation. Closing her eyes, she waited for a knock.

None came. Tears welled in her eyes as his footsteps retreated. He went into his own cabin and slammed the door.

The days passed, with no sign of the wreck. Tension was high; tempers were short as the men reacted to the stress. Francisco became quiet, brooding.

But he watched her. She could feel it everywhere she went. It was as before, when he was always hovering nearby, waiting.

Everyone was waiting. It was as if the *Fortuna* were suspended at the edge of a huge waterfall, the white water rushing past as the boat teetered. Where was the *Corazón*? Where was their lady of the sea?

Another long day was dragging by. Jane, clad in her Mickey Mouse T-shirt and a pair of blue shorts, sat on the deck beside Ricardo, a huge bowl of shrimp between them. Mechanically Jane shelled a large one and dropped it into another bowl filled with water.

Francisco sat in the navigation cabin, the door held open with a rock. He squatted in front of the magnetometer display, calling out the numbers in a low, tight voice.

Jane swallowed. This distance between them was so painful. Her thoughts were filled with the feel of his hands on her body, the way his eyes had flamed with desire that last night together, his soft voice as he talked of the love Spanish men have for their women. The men wept if their flowers withered. They wept. . . .

How did it happen? she asked herself miserably. How did I fall in love with him? He thinks so little of me. The barbs he had flung at her still dripped poison into her heart.

But she did love him. She loved his smile, his passion, and his wit. She loved him for having a dream and for protecting that dream with everything he possessed.

Ricardo was studying her. Reddening, she picked up another shrimp and managed to demolish it. The white meat fell from her hands in a clump, landing on the deck. Despairing, she scooped it up and deposited it with the discarded shells.

Francisco wiped his brow and rose to his feet. Motioning Ernesto over, he indicated that the man should watch the machine while his *jefe* took a break. Shoulders slumped, he meandered down the port side of the boat, staring out to sea.

Jane studied him, her anger dulled by his obvious misery. His time was running out. She had never seen him so despondent. Gone was the proud Latin male, preening before her, the furious, frustrated man lashing out with hateful accusations. In his place stood a fellow human being, worried and upset.

Plopping another cleaned shrimp into a ceramic bowl, she put down her knife and watched him. His broad shoulders were rigid, his knuckles white as he clutched the rail.

Ricardo said nothing when she wiped her hands on a towel and walked slowly toward the captain of her heart.

Joining him at the rail, she shared his silent vigil, begging the water to reveal the cache.

"Jane . . ." he murmured. "My little saboteur. I suppose I shouldn't blame you. You have a dream to protect, the same as I do."

At that, her fragile composure, the moment of tenderness, vanished. Her eyes blazing with anger, she shouted, "Goddammit, you self-righteous bastard!" I didn't say anything to him! I don't know why he said I did, but he was lying!"

He returned her look. "*Hostia,* you swear like a sailor! And have you no loyalty to the man who saved your school from debt?"

"I would have saved it myself! I didn't ask him to! Good

Lord, I don't even know him! And I'll swear if I damn well please!''

"Not on my boat!"

"Yes, on your boat!" Her hands doubled into fists, and for a wild moment she thought about hitting him. But she gathered control of herself and moved away from him.

"Come back here! We need . . . I need . . ."

She kept walking. "Go to hell!"

A shrill wail pierced the air, like a foghorn on a tugboat. Jane gasped and whirled around.

"Don Francisco! *Ya! Lo tenemos*!" cried Ernesto. "Hans, *alto*!"

Francisco raced to the readout display. Jane ran after him. He clutched the gray box with both hands and stared at the square red numbers. Hans and Ernesto hooted with triumph and began to dance in a little circle.

A cry went up all over the boat. Ricardo raced toward them, his shrimp knife in his hand.

"Francisco?" Jane croaked. "Is it?"

He stared at her for a long, quiet moment. Slowly, as if in a dream, he nodded. "We have something," he hedged. "By the Virgin, we have something!"

But his calm pose lasted only a moment. Gathering her up his arms, he kissed her long and hard. "My lady! I've found my lady!"

"Yes," she breathed, willing the hurt to go away. She knew he was speaking of his other lady. "I'm glad. I really am."

He stared at her intently. "So am I, Juanita."

Then he left her, running to meet his mermaid.

The crew stood along the railing as Francisco prepared to go down alone. Carlos stood by with the metal detector that his *jefe* would guide through the water, searching for the object that had set off the magnetometer. The mechanic's

hands trembled as he held the machine, which looked something like a lawn mower.

Many hands were trembling in that moment. Some of the
men crossed themselves. Beside Jane, Ricardo murmured a
short prayer.

Francisco looked at her. His very being crackled with
emotion as their eyes met. "Do you wish me luck?" he asked
her.

Swallowing, she nodded. "I . . . I'll say a prayer," she
managed.

His face warmed with a secret, pleased smile. "God listens
to the prayers of good women," he said. "We'll show
Alejandro, eh?"

"Yes. We will." The still-lingering pain of their argument
rushed over her, but only for a second. There were other
things to feel now—incredible hope, exhilaration, the sense
of fulfillment of Francisco's destiny. Every good wish she
had ever harbored in her heart rose up and focused its power
on the magnificent pirate before her.

"Go with God," she said softly.

"*Gracias*. Jane, I . . ." Reaching around his neck, he
unclasped his golden medallion, coiling the heavy chain in
her hand. "I don't want to confuse the detector," he explained,
holding it out to her. He closed her fingers around it tightly.

"I'll take good care of it," she promised.

He hesitated, then put on his mask. She could still see his
dark eyes through the glass.

He slipped a pair of earphones over his curly hair, then
flipped over the side. Carlos lowered the magnetometer down
to him, and he disappeared.

The minutes ticked by. Jane craned her neck, straining to
pick out Francisco's form beneath the surface. No one dared
to move or breathe. Only the screeching of the seabirds and
the slapping of the water against the boat broke the taut
silence. Please, let it be, she pleaded, clenching the medallion.
Let him find his dream.

"He no do," Ricardo muttered, scratching his chin.

"Yes, he do," Jane breathed. "He's got to. He must."

The sun moved in the sky. Still there was no sign of Francisco. Jane knew he had plenty of air, plenty of time, but she couldn't help the anxiety that began to gnaw at her. What if something happened to him? What if he got hurt and couldn't surface? If his foot got stuck, as María's had?

She caught herself. She was being ridiculous. Francisco was an expert diver. There was no reason to worry. Yet the little fear pricked her just beneath the skin. This is how he feels about me, she thought, only more so, because he carries the guilt of his cousin's death, and because he's such a passionate man. If we ever did wind up together, he'd go through hell every time I dived.

"*Ya!*" Hans cried. "Don Francisco!"

Jane leaned over so far that she almost fell overboard. Behind her the men surged forward, some shouting, some quieter and more tense than ever.

Francisco's fist appeared before he surfaced. He was shaking it jubilantly. Then he burst through the water, raising his mask. "*Sí!*" he cried. "*Sí!*"

Jane covered her mouth with her hands. The others broke into wild cheering, laughing and slapping each other on the back. Their raised voices frightened the tenacious birds, who dipped and swirled like a hurricane as they flew away.

Bernardo and Carlos pulled Francisco up and carried him onto the deck. Ricardo grabbed the metal detector. The men embraced their captain, kissing him on both cheeks as they stripped him of his mask and earphones. A bottle of champagne popped open. A great bubbling torrent of it doused him. Laughing, shouting, he leaned his head back and opened his mouth, swallowing huge gulps of the sparkling wine.

Then he saw Jane. He wiped his face and took another drink, then handed the bottle to her.

"It might not be the *Corazón*," he warned, although everything about him shouted that he was sure he had found her.

"It might be anything—an old fishing trawler, a missing cargo vessel."

"But you don't think so," Jane said, smiling brilliantly.

He smiled back. "No. I don't think so." He turned to the men and spoke in quick, staccato Spanish. "We're going back down," he informed her.

She nodded wistfully.

Crossing his arms, he raised his brows. "So why do you stand there? Hurry and suit up!"

Her lips parted. She stared at him, dripping with salt water and champagne, his face flushed and happy. Was he serious? Did he really mean it?

"Jane, I know that you speak very good English," he said with mock confusion. "So it must be my fault that you don't understand. Let me try again. *El jefe*, he do. You do, too."

Beside him, Ricardo frowned, sure that they were making fun of him. Jane couldn't help but laugh, although it was from the pure joy of being asked to explore the wreck, and not because of Ricardo's discomfort.

"I do!" she cried ecstatically. "Oh, Francisco, thank you!"

"Don't thank me." He gave her a wry, crooked smile. "Thank Alejandro."

That gave her pause. Was he asking her only because of the dressing-down that Alejandro had given him? She was being permitted to join in to please Alejandro? Then perhaps she shouldn't go. She thought of their fight, of the bitter words. She certainly didn't want to ruin his moment of triumph.

How ironic, she thought. I finally get my way, and now I'm not so sure I want to take it. . . .

"Hurry," Francisco admonished. "I'm not in the mood for waiting."

"Francisco . . .," she began.

Scowling, he stood tall before her. "Jane, this is a direct order, which you promised to obey while you were under my command. Now, move your beautiful American bottom and get your tanks!''

She should have known better, of course. But she was disappointed when they reached the site where the metal detector had guided Francisco. All she saw were mounds of coral and sand—no barnacled masts, no treasure chests, nothing to distinguish this part of the Mediterranean from any of the rest of it.

But the men nodded excitedly, seeing things she could not. The lay of the mounds, the extraordinary number of fish hovering nearby—these things indicated the presence of a wreck, long buried, long forgotten.

Francisco swam ahead, holding the metal detector in front of him. Suddenly he waved his hand. They gathered around him, pointing at the dial on the crossbar he held.

Jane hovered on the perimeter. Francisco motioned her over and gestured for her to put on the earphones. Obeying, she started when she heard the fierce wailing, like some sea monster's baby demanding to be fed.

Nodding eagerly, she gave him back the earphones. But he handed them to Carlos, giving the man the detecting device as well. Then he took Jane's hand and led her farther down, closer to the swell of coral, protecting whatever lay underneath it like the lid of a giant sarcophagus. He patted it and crossed his fingers. In reply, she copied his movements.

Then he drew nearer. She felt herself stiffen as he reached a hand toward her. He drew back, aware of the change in her. In the gurgle of the bubbles they regarded each other.

I don't trust him, she thought dismally. I don't know what he thinks of me anymore, or why he let me come down, or anything. He was so quick to believe Alejandro over me. He was so icy and hateful. Is he just trying to placate Alejandro? Maybe his pride is wounded. He's not used to women standing up to him, swearing, and stalking off. Maybe he's tired of sleeping alone. . . .

Francisco grabbed her hand and pulled her toward him. At his touch, her confusion intensified, along with an almost overwhelming urge to stop thinking at all, to simply enjoy the pleasure he could bring her. His chest expanded as he reeled her in like a helpless fish dangling on the end of his line, lured by his kisses, his hard body, his eyes. . . .

But the others swam above them like a school of sharks massing for a feed. Their shadows crossed over Francisco's face. She wriggled away and swam toward the group. He didn't follow her. Instead, he continued his inspection of the mound of coral.

Later, they went back down with pickaxes and saws and began their attack on the coral. Jane worked beside Francisco, copying his movements, lugging the heavy, sharp pieces to a wicker basket attached to a large orange balloon. Periodically, one of the men would make the basket buoyant by placing an air hose inside the balloon, enlarging it, and making it lighter. Then he would swim it over to a place away from the work area, where he would dump the load and return with the empty basket for another.

The work was hard, tedious, and backbreaking. Yet Jane kept pace as best she could, steadily hacking at the huge masses that shielded the wreck from their view. Visibility was poor as sand and coral dust whirlpooled around her, but she knew that Francisco was watching her. The knowledge made her clumsy, but she persevered, swimming her clumps over to the basket. After Carlos showed her how to work the air hose, she even unloaded the basket itself, although the cumbersome load was hard to maneuver.

It began to grow dark. Francisco motioned everyone to the surface, where Ricardo and Ernesto waited. There were always two left on board to watch the compressors and to stand ready in case of an emergency. They had taken turns, though neither Francisco nor Jane had stood a topside watch yet.

Her muscles cried out when she struggled up the rope ladder. Her arms were so tired that it was all she could do to take off her tanks and ease them to the deck. Ricardo picked them up for her, and she thanked him with pathetic gratitude.

Francisco cocked his head. "Is this too much for you?" he asked.

"No," she replied quickly. "Not at all."

"*Bueno*. Then you'll go down again tomorrow." He handed Carlos his ax. "The work goes faster with more hands."

"Fast enough?" she asked.

"Who knows? Perhaps you'll be able to persuade Alejandro that we need more time." There was a strange look on his face, a mixture of grim determination and something else, something that softened his features. Then it was gone, replaced by a grudging bob of his head.

"You did well today. I was surprised."

"I was, too," she admitted.

He wrapped his fingers around her shoulders. She winced. "That bad, eh?"

"No, no, I'm fine."

"Let's go to my cabin," he ordered, his eyes flaring. "I'll give you a massage."

"No, I have to help Ricardo," she blurted. "I promised him that I would—"

Over his shoulder, he spoke to the little cook. The man shook his head.

"He doesn't need you," Francisco said. "I do."

His fingers were already soothing her weary sinews, melting her resistance so that the desire that lay dormant within her began to awaken. She looked up at him as he towered over her. Her corsair. The pirate of her heart.

"Jane," he murmured, "why do you fight me now? I've given you everything you wanted. Won't you give me what I want?"

What is it that you want? she almost asked. My heart, my influence with Alejandro, or my body? Or maybe all three?

"Come," he said, taking her hand. Silently he led her down the ladder to his cabin, his feet leaving wet footprints that she stepped in as she trailed behind him.

Though the air was balmy, Jane shivered as the breeze wafted through the open porthole above his bunk. They were both wet and salty, their bathing suits still dripping. Francisco peeled his off and hung it on the edge of a chair. He waited for her to do the same.

When she didn't, he perched on the edge of the bed and pulled her into his lap. With slow, hard strokes he rubbed her back, bending her forward with the pressure. She breathed deeply, her body stirring. She was aware of the coarse hair on his thighs, brushing against the backs of her legs, of his breath on her skin. But more than anything, she felt his growing tumescence through the flimsy fabric of her pink bathing-suit bottom.

"Tomorrow the work will be easier," he promised. "I want to spend part of the day looking through the next batches of coral. There might be artifacts." His fingers pressed against the muscles below her shoulder blades, and she jumped.

"Ah, a knot," he said, kneading the area. He shifted on the bed, his male hardness pushing against Jane's suit.

"My mother used to massage my back at night," he went on. "I had a hard job at the time. I would get spasms right here." He drew a line across her rib cage.

He didn't speak for a time. The cabin walls flared with red as the sun began to sink into the water. Gradually the magenta gave way to paler reds, then to a muted lavender, then the golden glow of the Mediterranean twilight.

Through it all, he moved his hands on her body, rubbing her back, arms, and neck. She could feel his tight abdomen brush against her back every so often. Ripples of longing fanned out from the base of her spine, making her more conscious than ever of the fact that he was naked and wanted her. Her muscles tightened at the thought of it, but his firm strokes forced them to relax again.

"Remember when you got your sunburn? How I massaged you with my mother's ointment?"

Without speaking, she nodded. He sighed.

"You were afraid of me then, too. Jane, why do you fear me so?"

She tried to jerk her head around, but her neck still was too sore.

"I'm not afraid of you," she countered. "That's silly."

"You're lying. To yourself more than to me, I think."

"No."

"Why do you fight pleasure so hard? Is it because you think you must always stand guard over yourself, so that no man will dominate you? Is that the way of women's liberation?"

Suddenly he pulled the straps off her shoulders and ran his fingers over the bare flesh. Bending his head, he kissed the right shoulder, then moved down her arm, leaving a trail of tingles in his wake.

"*Dios*, I want you," he whispered. "You know that I want you."

"Francisco," she pleaded, wanting to talk, not wanting to talk. There was magic in the air again, fragile and fleeting, and she was loath to destroy it with words.

He turned her around so that she was facing him, straddling him. With a sharp, quick movement, he unhooked her top and let it fall, exposing her breasts. The nipples were pointed and red as berries. Dropping his gaze to them, he covered them with his palms. His callused fingertips brushed the tan line of her skin.

"My mermaid," he murmured. "My lady. Jane, I know I'm foreign to you. I know I frighten you. But I can be gentle, my little rose. I can make you grow toward the sun. Let me do it. Come to me willingly. Come with passion, the way you did the night on the beach. There's no reason to be afraid of the fire that rages inside you. It will not burn you."

"I'm not afraid," she insisted, but she saw that her hands were shaking.

Francisco covered them with his and brought them to his face. "I can be gentle," he repeated. He lifted up her chin with his thumb and forefinger while his other hand caressed her neck. His hand traveled down her side, rounded the swell of her breast, clasping her small waist tenderly.

"Your body is so perfect. Do you remember the day you came aboard the *Fortuna*? When you tripped and I put my hands around your waist? I wanted to kiss you. I would have, if Carlos hadn't interrupted."

"Yes," she managed. "I remember."

"I thought you did." He moved from her waist to the small of her back, lingering there. "What else do you remember?"

"I . . ." She trailed off. She didn't want to talk; she was so afraid of ruining the moment. Even now, her doubts were rising again. He had changed too fast, too radically. One moment, they were at each others' throats. The next, they were in each other's arms. It didn't make sense.

"Jane, why do you grow cold against me?" he asked. "Is it the fight we had? *Hostia*, I am Spanish! We are emotional people. And I—"

"No," she said. "I . . . I'm just cold," she lied.

"Then I will warm you." His hands slid into her bathing-suit bottom and cupped her buttocks, separating them slightly, before he removed the bottom of the suit as well.

A blaze of heat shot through her and she collapsed against his chest. Francisco buried his face in her hair.

"Jane, I swore to be gentle. I swore not to frighten you. But if I don't take you now, I won't be able to control myself."

She thrilled at his words, her back arching as he pushed her legs open. Lifting her slightly, he eased himself inside her. Jane caught her breath as he immersed her in a roaring cascade of pleasure, hoisting her into his arms and leaning her back against the edge of his desk.

Then he took her with implacable, almost savage thrusts,

holding her wrists behind her as she writhed on the map-strewn desk. With each piercing, she grew more aroused, more greedy for the next, and the next. Francisco, bathed in a sheen of perspiration, groaned deep in his throat as he fought to satisfy her, to plunge into her so completely that she might be propelled into ecstasy, and he with her.

"Oh, God," she moaned, overcome. "Oh, God."

"Now," he commanded. "Go now!"

Her flesh obeyed him. Like a comet, she soared into the night sky, streaking past the stars and the planets. He was with her; she could dimly hear his cry as he climaxed inside her.

"*Te quiero*," he murmured. "*Te quiero, te adoro, te amo*." I want you. I adore you. I love you.

Jane caught her breath as she slowly came back to earth-bound reality. He had never said that he loved her before. She didn't think he would, if he didn't feel it.

Throwing back her head, she gazed up at him with hopeful eyes. Had he even realized what he had said?

Please let it be true, she prayed. Please let him say it again.

But his eyes were closed and his face was blank. He drooped over her, breathing hard, his hands still gripping her hips.

"Francisco," she whispered.

Opening his eyes, he smiled and lifted her off the desk. Then he settled her onto his bunk. Sitting beside her, he toyed with her hair.

"Does this mean we're friends again?" he asked teasingly.

Friends. Weren't they more? She couldn't help the tumult she felt at his words.

"I suppose so," she said vaguely.

"You suppose so?" he asked, his brows arching. "Do you normally sleep with men who aren't your friends?"

Her lips parted. "That was unkind."

He sighed. "It was meant to be a joke. Forgive me, *maja*."

"All right," she said, but she knew that she hadn't. If he could make love to her, still believing she had betrayed him, then he must not feel the words he had cried.

"My Jane," he murmured, clasping her breast. She looked up at him. "Let's call a truce," he said. "Let's forget about Alejandro. *Hombre*, if only we'd met somewhere else . . ."

But we didn't, she thought sadly. We didn't.

He leaned over and kissed her. "I missed you, *mi amor*." His face was somber. "More than I thought possible."

"Did you?" she asked. He nodded.

Maybe she was wrong about him. She was judging him as harshly as he had judged her. Slowly she put her arms around him.

"I missed you, too."

"Then you'll agree to a truce?"

"Yes." She pressed her face against his. They held each other, savoring their reunion.

"It would have been life's greatest irony," he whispered, "to lose you the day that I found *El Corazón*!" He kissed her cheek. "Thank you, *mi amor*, for weathering my storm."

She sighed. Yes, she had weathered his. Now, could she weather her own?

Chapter Eight

❧

"Jane, have you found anything?"

Jane and Francisco sat hunched over a white canvas tarp onto which several piles of coral and rocks had been deposited by the divers. Jane's fingers were sore from cracking apart the sharp coral and breaking the pieces into smaller bits. They had been examining the haul for over an hour, searching for coins, nails, fragments of pottery—anything that would indicate the presence of a wreck.

Sighing, she shook her head. "No. I thought I had a piece of silver, but it was just an old barnacle."

He smiled. "So did I. Mine was simply a play of the light." He reached for another piece of coral. "It's hot today, no?"

"Yes. Very." She arched her back. "I thought you said the work today would be easier. I'd rather be diving."

His smile faded. "You like to dive very much, don't you?"

"Yes. It's the most important thing in my life." Except for him. The thought rushed in like a wave—impossible to stop or to ignore.

But the sea, her other lover, was constant. It would never leave her, never hurt her, unlike a man. Unlike Francisco.

She peered up at him through her lashes. He was considering her reply, scratching his forehead beneath the dark blue bandanna that he had rolled into a sweatband around his head. It gave him a decidedly roguish air, lending a dash of style to his cutoffs and T-shirt.

Jane was his twin, except that her headband was of pink terry cloth and she was barefoot, while Francisco wore sneakers with no socks. They had spent a pleasant hour working side by side, but now Jane could feel the tension beginning to brew between them.

The subject of diving brought it on every time. She wondered if Francisco had assigned her to this job because he regretted his impulsive invitation of yesterday. Perhaps he was sweetening the task by staying with her himself. She couldn't imagine that he'd rather be doing this than working below with the others.

If they ever did have a lasting relationship, she realized, they would have to work through this. She understood his fears for her, and the reason for them. But she couldn't imagine a life without her world beneath the waves. She'd be a beached mermaid, unable to exist.

But of course, there was no guarantee that their affair would outlast the hunt. She cracked opened another rock and dug through the bits and pieces. The only one convinced of that was Celia, who was so in love with the idea of love that she chose to overlook her husband's grievous shortcomings. Still, she couldn't help but think of it, just as she hadn't been able to stifle her daydream of walking down the aisle of San Pedro as Francisco's bride.

Francisco leaned over and kissed her cheek. "Thank you for forgiving me, *maja*. I know I've been a monster."

"Oh, no," she said quickly.

He chuckled. "Oh, yes. Last night was magic. Thank you for it."

"The pleasure was mine." She basked in his smile, echoing it on her lips. She laid her hand on his knee.

He groaned. "You aggressive American," he murmured. "Are you trying to seduce me?"

"Who needs to seduce Don Juan?" she taunted, and he laughed.

"Beauty and brains, too. How did I get so lucky?"

She basked in his compliment. "Flattery, *señor*, will get you everywhere."

"Now, Jane, we must work," he said with mock sternness. "After all, we're playing with your partner's money."

His words bruised her barely healed wound. "It's not a game to you," she said quietly.

"This is dangerous territory," he said. "Let's talk of other things. Like the liberation of women."

She dropped the rock bits into the discard pile. "That's not dangerous?"

Reaching for a piece of coral, Francisco shrugged. "Well, I'm curious about it. Of course, we have a women's movement in Spain, too, but they look to you Americans as their model. So you're the heart of the problem—ah, I mean, the situation."

"That's better," she said. "We'll have you converted yet, *señor*!"

"I'd be an outcast!" he protested theatrically. "I can hear it now: 'Where's old Pontalba? Oh, he's in his apron, changing diapers while his wife is off at the steel factory!' "

"If you were an American man, I'd take offense at that," she observed. "I guess I can forgive you more easily because you're just a foreigner who doesn't know any better."

He drew his hand up her thigh. "That's not why you forgive me," he drawled. She flushed.

"And I wouldn't leave my children," she added.

Looking surprised, he stopped breaking the coral and eyed her. "No? But I thought that was what women's liberation was about!"

"You see? You don't know anything about it! It's about choices. I wouldn't choose to work." Her voice grew soft. "I was left alone so much. I know what it feels like. I wouldn't want a child of mine to go through that."

His face lit up. "*Olé*, Jane. I like that very much."

They looked at each other, their eyes widening as if they were surprised at something. Jane felt a blanket of red cover her face. Oh, God, he's thinking what I'm thinking, she realized. He's thinking about us, and marriage, and children.

He gestured to a rock beside her knee. "Let me see that piece a moment," he said, holding out his hand. "It has an interesting shape."

She complied, watching as he turned it over, her heart racing. His hands were unsteady, as if he'd received a shock.

"With a little more evenness, this could have been a ballast stone," he said. "But it isn't." He set it on the tarp with the other debris they'd already checked. "*Hostia*, I'm thirsty. Would you like some sangría?"

"Is there any more pineapple juice? I'd rather have that."

"I'll check."

As he stood, his knees cracked. He made a face. "*Ay*, I'm getting old. Celia says I need a woman to take care of me now that my youth is gone." He gave her a wolfish grin. "Don't you feel sorry for me, waiting on you like a slave? After all, you are the woman. You should be getting me a drink!"

"Don't ruin the day," she said mournfully, although inwardly his words made her heart beat faster. They had never talked like this before. Was he wondering about their future, too?

He ambled across the deck, the well-defined muscles shifting in his legs as he moved. Jane watched him go, feeling proud and possessive and more than a little confused. Everything had begun to change since the discovery of the wreck. Correction: he had changed. Whereas he had so recently believed the very worst of her, now he seemed to see only the best. Was this just another shifting of the wind of his violent emotions? Or did it signal something permanent, some new feeling about her?

He returned, handing her a cup of sweet pineapple juice

and a handful of strawberries. "From your boyfriend," he said. "If this keeps up, I'll have to challenge him to a duel!"

"Ever the romantic," she teased. "I'll tell Ricardo to be more discreet from now on."

"Please. My Latin soul is very jealous." He studied her as he drank, his lashes half-hiding his deep-set eyes. It was as if he hypnotized her when he looked at her like that.

And he? What did it take to hypnotize Francisco Miguel de la Martín Pontalba? Had she done it without knowing it?

"We've worked all day and we haven't found a thing," she blurted, running from her own thoughts.

He tousled her curls. "Patience. I know we'll get something. If not today, then tomorrow."

"*Mañana*," she drawled. "You Latin types. How do you ever accomplish anything?"

He bumped her with his elbow, nearly spilling her drink. "Watch yourself, you barbaric American! My country ruled an empire before yours was even discovered!" He leaned back on his arm and chuckled.

"Ah, civilized Spain," she said expansively. "Home of the Inquisition. And the bullfight. Nothing barbaric there."

"You're right, *señorita*. There is nothing barbaric about the bullfight. It's an ancient ritual, created by the Minoans and the Cretes. The bulls and the matadors do the dance of bravery and death together. It's an honorable thing."

Holding her cup in her left hand, she chipped a piece of coral with a small hammer. "Well, I suppose I shouldn't be too critical. I've never been to a bullfight."

"And you live in San Diego?" he asked, surprised. "But you're right next to Tijuana! They have a very nice ring, I hear."

She made a moue of apology. "It never struck me as something I wanted to do. You know how it is when you live somewhere. You never see half the things that tourists do. Whenever I drive across the border, I just go shopping."

"We'll have to change that," he said. "I'll take you to the

ring in Madrid. It's one of the largest in the world. There's nothing like the spectacle of opening day! You'll love it!''

"And when is opening day?"

He stopped. "I forgot," he murmured. "You'll be gone by then."

Her heart clutched. "Well," she said vaguely, "I can always go to the one in Tijuana."

"Maybe one day you'll return to Spain."

Suddenly her fingers felt numb. Sadness flooded through her, its chilly waves spreading over her heart and closing her throat. The thought of leaving him and his world was almost more than she could bear. In the bright, sunlit day, it seemed impossible that this would not last forever. But they had less than seven weeks left, seven days times seven.

It was just as well, she thought, if he didn't share her feelings, if he could speak of their parting as lightly as if he were discussing what they were going to have for dinner. Like a litany, she began to repeat the old singsong words of comfort—he was too macho; he wouldn't let her continue her diving career; she would never be the docile wife he would want . . .

And yet, if he asked her, if he said, "Juanita, will you be my *mujer*, my wife, the mother of my children?"

His children. His water babies. Little dark-headed boys and honey-haired girls, bobbing in the sea beside their proud papa. She could see him tossing a squealing child into the air and catching it in his loving arms, the child he was never allowed to be because he had to become a man so soon.

Oh, if he asked her, she would say . . .

"Jane, are you all right?" he asked, moving closer. The hairs on his arm brushed hers, sending a jolt through her that shook her from her reverie.

"Yes. I was just thinking about how little time we have left. For the hunt, I mean."

He drained his glass, turning away as he did so. "*Sí*, it bothers me too. If this isn't the *Corazón*, and we don't discover that soon, we won't have time to look elsewhere. Unless you can sweet-talk Alejandro into giving us more money."

Alejandro again. His very name cast a cloud over her. Francisco couldn't be manipulating her just to keep his partner at bay, could he? His words of love, his tenderness— were they all designed to placate Alejandro? Were they his proof that he had "reformed"?

He couldn't be just using her; he just couldn't. It would be too cruel, too devious. Francisco wasn't a cruel man.

But he was a driven man. One who would do almost anything to get what he wanted. And he wanted the *Corazón*.

Francisco took the coral out of her hands and pressed her fingers to his lips.

"I want you. Now," he whispered. "Let's go below."

"But our work—"

"Now. And then we'll work." He rose, pulling her with him.

Their lovemaking was fierce, impassioned. Francisco made no attempt to be gentle. It was as if he couldn't get enough of her. Her body throbbed all over from his knowing caresses, fanning her into a bonfire of erotic heat. Their coupling was uncontrollable, like a storm at sea. She was the tempestuous wind, he the volatile lightning. They raged together into a hurricane of impulses and emotions, past thought, past anything Jane had ever felt before. Higher and higher they rose, like a tidal wave, until release crashed over them in a tumult and they rested against each other,

"Ah, my rose," he murmured as he drifted off to sleep. "It's so new to me."

"What is?" she whispered, feeling the gentle rise of his chest against her breasts, his hands coiled in her hair.

But he didn't answer. He was already asleep.

He was gone when she woke. Quickly she dressed, then thought better of it and put her suit on under her clothes. If he asked her to dive this afternoon, she'd be ready.

She went topside, to find that he wasn't on deck.

"He do," Ricardo explained, pantomiming cracking open coral and rocks, as they had done that morning. Jane nodded, savoring a cup of *café con leche*. She'd acquired quite a taste for it. Back home, she drank her coffee black.

"This tastes very good," she said in Spanish. She smiled proudly. Her college studies were coming back to her. Every day, it seemed she could understand a little more of what was being said around her.

Ricardo frowned. "English only," he admonished. "You say."

"I'm sorry," she apologized. She had promised to speak only English with him. It hadn't done much good. He was one of those people who just couldn't seem to learn foreign languages. She was surpassing him in that department.

"*Bueno, bueno,*" Ricardo assured her.

She wagged a finger at him. "English only, *amigo*." He clapped his head and exhaled between his jack-o'-lantern teeth.

Whistling, he opened a jar of olives and plopped them into a bowl. Next, he added some vinegar and olive oil. Jane watched him as she drank her coffee. He smiled at her, stirring the mixture with a wooden spoon.

"I'm going to look for Don Francisco," she said. He nodded, waving as he added some garlic to the bowl.

She sauntered outside with her cup, watching the men check the air hose. Carlos waved, wishing her a good day. The others did likewise. There had been a marked change in their attitude since yesterday's dive. She wondered how much of it had to do with their real feelings and how much was determined by the fact that *el jefe* had accepted her as one of the crew.

"*Buenos días, señorita,*" Hans said cordially. He had been the one most opposed to her. She could still see his glowering face on that first day.

"*Buenos días,*" she replied, smiling. He smiled back and made a place for her beside him on the deck.

Well, why not? she thought, and began to walk toward him.

Just then, Francisco bounded around the corner and hoisted her over his shoulder. The crew began to laugh and hoot.

"What are you doing?" she cried, flailing. Her coffee cup clattered to the deck.

Francisco raced to the starboard side, holding her tight.

"Remember that night you challenged me to catch you?" he asked. "The night you cheated by jumping overboard?" He dropped her into his arms and held her out over the water.

"Francisco! Don't!"

The men were clapping in unison, chanting "Let go! Let go!" in Spanish.

Jane struggled, clinging to him. "You put them up to being nice to me!" she accused. "Just so you could play this dirty trick!"

"What are you talking about? I saw you come out of the galley and I made my move!"

"But Hans smiled and—"

"Are you flirting with my men again?" he demanded, and he let go of her. She crashed into the water in an inelegant sprawl.

"I told you not to be so bold!" he shouted, genuinely angry. "Juanita, you must learn to listen to me!"

"Don't call me Juanita!" she bellowed, sputtering. Then she ducked beneath the water and began to take off her clothes.

Francisco watched with horror. "What are you doing? Are you insane? My men will see you!"

"Come and stop me, then," she challenged, hiding her bathing suit from his view.

"You . . . you . . . *American!*" he growled, ripping off his T-shirt and jumping in after her.

She swam away, giggling. Francisco came after her. Above

them, the men egged her on, yelling as if they were at a swim meet.

"Faster! Faster!" they called. Francisco's fingers brushed her heel; a boost of speed propelled her on, narrowly escaping him as he lunged behind her.

"*Ya, maja!*" Carlos called. "*Más rápido!*"

He was closing in. Attempting a feint, she dived beneath the water and made a move to the right, then quickly switched direction and began a frantic bid for distance to the left.

But he was too quick for her. He grabbed her feet and pulled her under, yanking her clothes out of her hands.

"You have on your suit!" he cried. "You lied to me!"

"No, I didn't," she said triumphantly. "You're just so hotheaded—"

"Hotheaded!" he shouted. "I am not!"

Jane's mouth began to twitch. Francisco saw it. He sighed. "*Bueno*, perhaps a little."

"Yes, Francisco. Just a little."

He tied her shirt and shorts together and wrapped them around his waist. "We're not going to get anything done today," he said.

"Of course we are," she replied.

His eyes filled with fire. "Not if you continue to entice me, *niña*." Taking her hand, he pressed it against him, so that she felt his desire.

She flushed. He brought her hand to his lips and kissed each finger. "Now, what's this about Hans?"

"Honestly, Francisco! You act like a medieval lord! He was just being friendly. All he did was offer me a seat beside him!"

"How many times do I have to tell you that Spanish men don't know how to be friendly to women? We have hot blood, Jane. You shouldn't toy with them!"

She scowled at him, tossing back her dripping hair. "That's the most ridiculous thing I ever heard! Do you think Ricardo's scheming to get into my pants?"

He was clearly shocked. "Don't speak like that," he snapped. "You're a lady. Don't talk like a *puta*."

"Captain Pontalba, I'll speak as I please! My vocabulary is none of your business!"

"Don't push me, woman! I'm trying to remember that you're a foreigner, but I'm this close to losing my temper!" He glided toward her menacingly.

Suddenly she was afraid of him. She'd forgotten his fierce temper, quick to explode. "Don't you badger me!" she shouted. "I'm sure Alejandro would be very interested to hear . . ."

That brought him up short. He stared at her, and she knew she had said the worst thing possible.

"I'm sorry," she blurted. "That's not true and I shouldn't have said it. You can't really think that I run to him with reports on you! I was just angry. I knew it would upset you, so I said it. I'm *sorry*."

He appraised her. "I don't know what to think," he said slowly. "Sometimes I . . ." He stopped, a puzzled expression knitting his heavy brows together. Sliding his arm around her waist, he kissed the side of her neck. "Forgive me, *mi amor*. These days I'm moving through uncharted waters."

"I understand. But it's going well, don't you think?" Her heart was still pounding from the chase and the argument; now her pulse quickened from the feel of his flesh against hers.

She saw that her words had confused him. "The digging, I mean. The search."

"Ah, that," he said, as if it were unimportant. Now it was her turn to feel puzzled.

"Let's go back now," he said. "We've got to get to work."

They returned to their piles of rock and coral. Francisco fetched more pineapple juice for her and sangría for himself. He laughed easily, joking and teasing with her. It was as if their argument had never occurred.

Hans meandered over, speaking to Jane in slow, measured Spanish. She answered him gingerly, eyeing Francisco, but now he took the man's overtures of friendship in stride. He even left the two of them alone while he went in search of another hammer.

It was such a switch from his temper tantrum that Jane felt uneasy. She remembered their first nights of love, and how tender and adoring he had been. Then the day would follow, and he would play the tyrant, as if the night had never occurred. It seemed to be happening all over again. He vacillated from captain to lover and back again, and she didn't understand what caused the change.

Hans wandered off when Francisco came back. He sat cross-legged beside her. "This is a better hammer," he said. "I don't know why I didn't use it sooner." Tapping a rock gently, he mumbled to himself in Spanish. "Dammit," he swore, as the rock cracked apart and there was nothing inside but more rock. "Alejandro is crazy." Sighing, he dropped it and picked up his sangría. "Let's dive," he suggested. "Ernesto and Ramón can work on these for a while."

She studied him. He seemed to have no reluctance when it came to allowing her to go down. Why? Before, he would have fought her so hard . . .

"All right," she said.

His hands closed over hers. "Jane, what's wrong? I thought it would please you to dive with me."

"Oh, it does," she said quickly. "There's nothing wrong."

He shifted his weight. "You're such a terrible liar. I may not have a woman's intuition, but I'm not blind. Please, Jane, won't you tell me what it is?"

She regarded him. He looked so earnest, so caring. Dared she tell him? What would he say? Would he laugh and try to cajole her into passing off her fears as nothing?

"Please, my rose." He stood, pulling her up with him.

They made their way to the bow, away from the hum of the air compressor, which fed the hose used to lift the wicker basket's orange balloon. For a moment they both stared out to sea, watching the birds and the waves. Then Francisco touched her arm. "Look. Dolphins."

A school of five of them, sleek and shiny, leapfrogged through the water. They squawked at each other in their funny voices, frolicking like children.

Again the image of Francisco and his babies rose in her mind. "Francisco . . ." she began. He turned to her, waiting. She looked back at the dolphins, trying to frame her questions. She was stalling; what she wanted to know was simple enough to say.

"Are you in trouble?" he asked softly. "I should have asked, I suppose. But I assumed you were taking care of it. You're so independent and all. You're American."

She was taken aback. All that talk of children must have put this into his head. Putting her hands on her hips, she whirled on him. "Yes, all American women start taking the pill at age twelve. Then we can hop into bed with anybody at the drop of a hat!"

"I didn't mean it that way," he snapped, drawing himself up.

"Well, I'm not in trouble," she said. "So you can relax."

"*Ay, niña,* don't be so harsh," he said, putting his arm around her. "I was trying to do the right thing. We have a barrier of culture between us sometimes. We see things so differently."

"Yes, we do." Taking a deep breath, she undraped his arm and faced him squarely. "I have to know something. Are you letting me dive and being so . . . nice . . . all of a sudden because you want me on your side instead of Alejandro's? Because you think that I'd really go to him and . . ."

The look on his face was one of pure shock. Even the sudden approach of the dolphins didn't stir him from his surprise as he stared at her. It was a look that made her want to laugh for joy.

"Jane, I'm insulted," he said, regaining a measure of his composure. "I'm not a . . . what do you say, a . . . *gigolo!*"

"Then why are you suddenly letting me dive all the time? You used be so scared—so insistent," she amended, realizing that she'd almost told him she knew about María. "What changed your mind?"

He watched the dolphins, his face growing serious. He didn't speak for a long time. When he did, his face was blank, a mask. "Alejandro very wisely pointed out that I needed your help," he said simply. "With the time so short, I had to admit that. And you have been helpful."

"Oh." She, too, turned her attention to the dolphins. It was easier to hide her disappointment that way, without looking at his sculptured features.

What had she expected? That he throw himself on his knees and proclaim that he now saw her as an equal and that he loved her for it with all his heart? That he had seen through the folly of his pride and wanted her with him, no matter what he was doing?

Yes, she thought, that's exactly what she did want. And what she had been foolish enough to hope for.

"Let's get our gear," he said. Then he smiled. "Are you satisfied now?"

"Oh, yes. Thank you, Francisco."

"*De nada*, Jane." They walked back. This time, he didn't hold her hand. He walked beside her, his thoughts elsewhere.

Suddenly he turned to her. "Jane," he said, "you're a beautiful woman. I cherish your hair on my pillow when I wake up." Bending down, he planted a chaste kiss on her lips. Caught off guard, she closed her eyes and savored the sweetness of his kiss.

His arms stole around her. He said something in Spanish, then pressed her close. He was troubled; she could see it in his eyes. The were black and depthless, like the deepest waters of the ocean.

"Who are you?" he asked her. "Are you my mermaid, come to haunt me?"

She frowned. "Haunt you?" The word hurt her; it made her feel unwelcome.

He gave her a weak smile. "Sometimes my English isn't very good."

That was a lie, of course. He spoke it beautifully. But she said nothing. As they walked past the tarp, she nudged a piece of coral with her toe. "I'll be the first to find treasure," she boasted, hiding her consternation behind an air of false bravado.

"Too late," he said cryptically.

It was a good dive. Jane hacked at the coral with all her might, taking her turn at filling the orange balloon and sending the basket to the surface, where Ernesto retrieved it.

As she labored, she noticed that the men weren't avoiding her as much. Carlos shared tools with her, and José Luis helped her carry the heaviest pieces to the basket. They worked closely together like a team. Jane smiled in silent gratitude. At last the "No Girls Allowed" sign was coming off the door.

When they surfaced for the day, Hans patted her on the back and told her, "*Muy bueno!*" The others nodded, praising her, passing a shot of whiskey her way. She drank, coughing, and they chuckled and pressed her to take another drink.

The sun was setting on the water, tinting it with ripples of silver and magenta. Under the mauve sky, Jane laughed with her fellow crewmates, pleased with the world. They had changed, Francisco had changed.

And she? She had changed, too. Love had mellowed her. Never had she felt so peaceful, so relaxed. All was very right with her tonight.

They ate supper. Francisco took his to the navigation cabin, explaining that he needed to study some charts. She nodded, knowing he would come for her later. So she ate her *langostino* leisurely and recounted the day's events in her crude but effective Spanish.

"I thought I'd drop that big rock!" she exclaimed as Hans indicated the size of the boulder the two of them had moved.

"*Ay, no,* you're strong. For a woman," Bernardo said.

She didn't take offense. She knew he meant well by his comment.

They talked on. The men drank more whiskey. Jane stuck to sangría, amused by the fact that, as they drank more, they began to brag more. Soon, rocks that had been as big as oranges were now the size of basketballs. Coral that had broken loose in five strokes took twenty to break off.

Francisco still didn't emerge from the cabin. A trifle disappointed, she finally bade her new friends good night and made her way down the ladder. Automatically, she headed for his door. Then she remembered all his admonitions not to be so bold. Thinking to please him, she went into her own cabin and undressed, crawling naked beneath the light sheet.

The stars twinkled on the water. She tossed in the balmy, moist night, waiting for her lover. With each creak of the boat, her body tensed, anticipating the pleasure he would evoke in every part, every cell.

The crew grew noisier, their voices carried by the water. They were arguing about something, but she couldn't figure it out. Slurred by drink, the words were hard to decipher.

Finally she sighed and sat up. Francisco should call it quits for the night. The day's work had been hard, and tomorrow promised to be no different. And she was hungry for his touch. . . . Dressing in her track shorts and Burton Diving shirt, she climbed the ladder and walked toward the navigation cabin.

"Mickey Mouse, how d'you do," Ricardo greeted her from the galley. He was doing the dishes. Jane lounged in the doorway, watching. Then she went in, picking up a dishrag and drying the silverware. She'd give Francisco a few more minutes.

"I'm fine. Thank you for the good dinner."

"Ah." He bobbed his head. "You welcome."

Near the stern, the men were talking and laughing. She could make out pieces of the conversation. They were daydreaming about what they would do with their shares of the booty. One would buy a car. She was pretty sure one said he would put it in the bank. The others teased him a lot about that.

"Not me!" Carlos boomed. "I'm going to spend it on wine and women!"

Jane shook her head and put the forks in a drawer. These Latins.

"Lots of women, like Don Francisco!" Carlos went on. "One in every city!"

She flushed. Ricardo cleared his throat and walked toward the galley door.

"No, please," she said. He started to go out, but Jane held out her hand.

"Hmmph," he muttered, returning to his post.

Carlos said something else that Jane couldn't understand, but Ricardo turned scarlet.

She turned to him. "What?"

He shook his head and plunged his hands into the soapy water so furiously that some of the suds sloshed over the front of his apron.

"Ricardo, what did he say?"

He washed another plate and slammed it in the drainer.

"Like the American *señorita! Hostia*, what a body! I'd like to . . ." Carlos used words Jane didn't know. She was sure she'd never have learned them in school. Ricardo's cheeks were blazing; he wouldn't even look at her.

"Esperanza de Anza, Valencia. Rosa Rodrigues, Madrid . . ." Carlos chortled.

"Hortensia Bauza, Palma," Hans took up the count. "Juana Burton!"

"*Olé, jefe!*" They were laughing uproariously.

"Oh, God." Jane's stomach felt like lead. He had a string of women! And Hortensia! Could it be? She remembered his hand on her arm, the looks they had given each other.

"*Sí*, Señorita Burton!" someone cried. The men laughed.

Jane lurched toward the door, seeking escape. How could they talk about her like this? How could they tell her the awful truth in such a hateful, hurting way?

I'm nothing to him, she thought wildly. Nothing but one of his conquests. I've been so blind, so stupid!

"Please, *señorita*, I to Don Francisco," Ricardo told her.

She waved him back. "No, Ricardo. Don't. Please don't let him know I heard this!"

Just then they heard a door burst open and footfalls on the deck. They came from the direction of the navigation cabin.

"*Idiotas*!" Francisco bellowed. He sounded livid. He began to yell at the men in rapid-fire Spanish. She heard a crack, then another, and another. Ricardo paled.

"Don Francisco," he said, punching the air in front of him.

It was too much. Jane fled the galley, flew down the ladder, and locked herself in her room. Above her, Francisco's voice shook the very timbers of the boat, echoing out to sea.

She stood rigid. Was it true? Was she just part of a harem of his, his current toy, his amusement? Had there been nothing more to it than that?

She felt so foolish, so . . . sappy. Oh, if only she'd listened to Chuck and Alejandro! They were right; she couldn't handle him. She didn't understand him; she never had. Was he laughing at her, too?

Her doorknob rattled. She couldn't face him now. She just couldn't.

But the door opened. Francisco stood in the doorway, shrouded in darkness. He shut the door behind him and came into the room. "I'm sorry for this," he said, his voice low. "I wish you didn't understand my language. What they said was unforgivable."

"Well, it was true, wasn't it?" she blurted, trying to sound light and casual. But her throaty rasp betrayed the fact that she had been crying.

"They had no right to discuss our personal affairs. I've punished them . . ." His voice trailed off.

"I'm surprised you brought Esperanza on board," she went on, forcing herself not to sound bitter. "Wouldn't she have been jealous of me?"

He sat down beside her. "Jane, you know that I've had other women."

Her heart began to thunder in her chest as an icy despair began to seep into her veins. Before he said it, she knew what he was going to say: it was true; she was just part of a harem. And she had dreamed of weddings and babies!

"My . . . appetite is not easily satisfied."

She reeled. This must be what it feels like, she thought, to discover that your husband has been unfaithful. This must be what Celia feels like. Hideous, miserable, mortified.

"Did you sleep with Hortensia?" she asked, keeping her voice steady.

He hesitated. "Tensia is a married woman."

"Emilio's a married man," she countered, fully aware that he hadn't answered her question. "You do know that he's cheating on Celia, don't you?"

Taking her hand, he pressed it to his lips. "She understands. She loves him."

"And that's enough?"

"*Sí*. For a Spanish woman."

Oh, God, her heart sobbed. Oh, Francisco! She was the one who had played the romantic, not he! She'd been living in a fairy tale ever since she had first fallen into his arms!

"Well, we're not married. You certainly don't owe me any loyalty." She laughed shakily. "And as you pointed out, I'm a modern American woman." Whose heart is breaking, she thought. Who wishes she'd never left her heart unguarded for a conquistador like you to break. Who is fighting back the tears with every ounce of determination she can muster.

Chapter Nine

꙳

Francisco sat beside Jane for a long time without speaking. The *Fortuna* groaned and creaked, punctuating the silence.

Finally he sighed. "Then you understand?"

Jane gripped the edge of the bed with both hands. Her world was crashing down around her shoulders, and he was asking if she understood! If only she didn't! If only she had been kept in blissful ignorance. Francisco wasn't hers, had never been. Would never be.

"Oh, well, I suppose if we . . . meant a lot to each other, it might be hard for me to take. But since our time together is short . . ." She swallowed, praying he would leave. She couldn't sit here calmly discussing his other women, hiding her true feelings for the sake of her pride. Thank God he had no idea of the pain he was causing her.

"I suppose I do understand. After all, we're two mature people. We knew what we were doing."

"I didn't think you would understand," he said, and there was a strangeness to his voice. He sounded almost . . . disappointed? Angry? She couldn't tell. Her ears were ringing. She was so shaken that she could scarcely make out what he was saying.

"You see, love and sex are not the same to a Latin man."

And theirs was a relationship based upon sex, he was saying. She crossed her arms, hoping he wouldn't be able to see how she was struggling not to break down in front of him.

"How convenient," she said evenly.

"Not really," he replied. "It's just the way we are."

"Like Emilio?"

"What do you mean?"

"I'm talking about his love for his little flower, Celia. You know, the one he's nurturing. The one he'd weep over if she . . wilted."

"Emilio loves Celia very much. He worships the ground he walks on."

"He has an interesting way of showing it," she retorted. 'In America, they'd probably get divorced over it!"

"We are Catholics, Jane. We marry for life. So a man . . . and a woman . . . must be very sure." In the dim light, she could see his profile as he spoke, so perfect, so noble, so heartless.

"Celia must be filled with regret," she observed.

"Ah, no. She counts herself the luckiest woman in Spain. She and Emilio have a good marriage."

Jane opened her mouth to argue, but she had to concede that Celia herself had said much the same thing. But how could they, when her husband was sleeping around? The whole idea was repugnant to her.

"You said once that there was a cultural barrier between us. You were right, Francisco. I wouldn't be able to take the knowledge that my . . . husband had a string of girlfriends."

He touched her hair. She closed her eyes, holding back the sob that welled at the back of her throat.

"Oh, Jane," he sighed. "How well did Alejandro know you before he sent you to me?"

"Not well at all," she managed.

"I'm not so sure." She felt his feathery touch as it followed the arch of her brow.

"In the morning, my men will apologize to you," he said. "I know it can't make up for what happened."

No, it couldn't. Because they weren't responsible for the agony she was going through. And his assumption that they were was making it worse. Had he no idea how he was wounding her?

Ah, but he was Latin. He was foreign. Was he capable of comprehending her point of view? She certainly didn't understand his. How could a man love a woman and still . . . ?

But Francisco didn't love her. He had never said so. Not really, except in one blind moment of passion.

And if he did? Could she accept him, wondering if he was with someone else whenever they were apart? Could she stand that kind of "love"?

"Hold me," she said quickly. "Just hold me, Francisco."

"*Ay, mi amor, mi querida.* Don't cry, my *rosita.*" He brushed his lips against her temple. "I would do anything to keep you from crying."

No you wouldn't, she thought miserably. But she sought his mouth with a desperation that frightened her, flinging her arms around his neck. How many others had kissed him in just the same way? How many women had wept over him? How many were eagerly awaiting his return? Hortensia . . .

"Go," she whispered, pressing her hands against his broad chest. "I can't. I need to be alone."

"No." He pushed her back against the bunk and buried his face between her breasts. "Jane, sweet Jane," he whispered "You're too beautiful for tears. Too fiery, my strong little American!"

No, I'm not, she wanted to sob. I'm so weak. If I had any sense at all, I'd make you leave. But I can't.

He held her for a long time, murmuring to her. She closed her eyes, drinking in the sound of his voice. How did Celia stand it? Knowing that Emilio murmured to others, whispering words of love. Knowing that Francisco . . .

She turned her head away, as if to block him out, but he eased her face toward his and kissed her. His lips lingered on hers while he tried to drive away her hurt feelings. At last Jane stirred beneath him, quickening.

He traced her brows with his little finger. "You've given

me a new world, *mi ángel*." Slowly, cautiously, he moved toward her breasts. When she didn't push him away, he fondled them through her T-shirt. "Do you feel how I want you? Do you know how I need you?"

He peeled the shirt over her chest, catching his breath at the sight of her rounded flesh covered by her silky bra. Jane moaned, unable to stop his exploration. I won't think of anything except the moment, she told herself. I won't think . . . .

He unfastened her bra and drew it away. Her nipples contracted in the cool air, stiffening as he circled them with his tongue. Pressing his head against her chest, he was like a child, suckling. She raked her fingers through his sable hair.

Right now, he's mine, she thought. It's enough. I'll make it be enough.

He sat up, bringing her with him, nipping the back of her neck. A thrill shot through her, and she arched, bringing her breasts toward his mouth.

"You want me still," he murmured. "My mermaid, you want me."

"Yes."

She helped him undress her; then he tore off his own clothes and lay beside her, drawing her to new heights of pleasure with his hands and his lips. He drew circles of flame over her stomach and hips as his tongue dueled with hers. Exploring her mouth, he found the sensitive insides of her lips and rubbed them gently with his callused fingers.

How many others? How many?

Don't think, her body pleaded. Take him. Take his pleasure.

Give to him, her heart demanded. Give him pleasure.

She obeyed, gathering him in her hands and feeling the hard heat of his masculine desire. He threw his head back and breathed between his teeth, making a hissing sound like some barbaric merman from the deep.

"Francisco, tell me what you want," she whispered.

"My sea rose," he moaned. "*Por Dios*, I am a fool!"

With a cry he took her, their bodies joining in a frenzy of healing passion, of soothing fire. They moved together, plunging into their own world of love, the kingdom only they could enter. Gliding through glowing golden rays of joy and delight, breathless, they were heedless of anything but intense, transporting ecstasy.

They surfaced together, in each other's arms. Waves of their echoed pleasure surged over them, then ebbed. They were left on the beach of the night to face each other. Jane turned away, her pain crashing over her all over again.

Francisco raised himself on his elbows and exhaled. His breath gentled on her neck like the wings of a butterfly.

"*Magnífico,*" he murmured, picking up a strand of hair and brushing it with his fingers. "You are my glory."

She said nothing, too miserable to speak. Can't I be enough? she wanted to ask. Aren't I woman enough?

He looked out the porthole, the stars glistening in his hair like a corona of light. He was as perfect as a statue.

She watched him silently, the tears streaming down her face, praying that in the morning she'd wake and discover it had all been an awful dream.

But it hadn't been a dream. As soon as the sun splashed on the walls of her cabin, she opened her swollen eyes and remembered.

Then she saw Francisco sitting beside her bed. He held out a cup of *café con leche*. "We're on our way to Mallorca," he said. "We've moved a lot of coral, but the sand is blowing in to fill the holes. We're going to build a device that will help us."

She was grateful to him for talking of other things. "I suppose that means another shopping trip with Celia," she said, trying not to spill the coffee as she took it from him. The mere touch of him unnerved her.

"Not this time. I'm putting you in charge of constructing it."

"Me!" Her eyes widened. "But the men—"

"Need to be taught a lesson. The same one I am learning," he added, lowering his voice.

"But I don't know anything about building treasure-hunting equipment! Francisco, it's crazy to expect—"

"Have I told you of the captain's share?" he cut in, his tone indicating a change of subject.

"No." She concentrated on her coffee, hoping he hadn't noticed her puffy eyes. When had he left her bed? Had he heard her crying in the night?

"*Bueno*. This is a good one, Jane. You'll like it." He settled back in the chair.

"You see, the captain always had a special cache of fortune for himself. He would hide it away where the crew would not find it. We Spaniards were notorious for it when we transported the Indian gold from the New World."

His eyes twinkled and he kissed the tip of her nose. "Why do you think so many captains went down with their ships?"

"Trying to save their secret share?" she guessed. He nodded.

"Often they would wrap it around their waists. With all that extra weight, they drowned!"

"The greedy things!"

"*Sí*." He leaned forward on his elbows. "There was no report of a captain's share on *El Corazón*."

"Do you think there is one?"

He thought for a moment. "I don't know. Alejandro thinks not, because the entire ransom belonged to the *corsaro*. He had no plans to share it with any of his crew."

He laced his fingers through hers. "But if I were that corsair, I'd hide some away, just in case. Pirate crews— whether they were protected by the Church or not—were dangerous, corrupt men. Those stories of mutiny and murder are all true. What is the saying in English? 'Dead men tell no tales.' So the less they knew of the fortune aboard *El Corazón*, the better for Fatima and her beloved."

"Then there might be even more treasure aboard."

"*Sí*, the best part of it." He tapped their entwined fingers against his lips. "We'll soon see."

"Are we close to finding something?" she asked.

He looked at her. "We have to be. I am, at any rate. Take it easy today, *sí*? you look . . . a little drawn. And tomorrow you'll need your strength to push those big men around!"

When she went topside, Francisco called the men over. They came to her one by one, doffing their caps, their heads hung. "I sorry," each said in English, then followed it with a lengthy apology in Spanish. Francisco stood by, his face grim, his arms crossed. They apologized to him, too.

She was shocked to see bruises on some of their faces. Hans sported a shiner; Carlos' lip was cut. She remembered the cracking noises she had heard, and Ricardo's explanation: "Don Francisco, he do." Because they were insulting her? Or because they were spilling the beans about his harem? Or both?

After everybody had filed past, Francisco gave the order to set a course for Mallorca. Then he explained that they were going to be building some equipment, and that Jane would be their *jefe* while they did it.

They were shocked. Even Ricardo was astonished. But not a single protest passed their lips. When Francisco instructed them to call her "Doña Jane," they nodded like docile cattle and waited for him to dismiss them.

They spent the next hour marking the work site with more orange balloons, making sure that they were securely fastened. If they floated away, it would be difficult for Francisco to relocate the exact area where they had been working.

He and Jane passed the time in the navigation cabin, where he showed her what he wanted her to build. It was called a "mailbox," and that's what it looked like—a large metal box. It was about fifteen feet wide, and it was shaped to direct the blast from the propellers downward, blowing away the sand from the site.

"It should be simple enough," he said. "Carlos and Hans have made one before."

"Then why not put one of them in charge?" she asked uneasily. "I really don't think this is a good idea."

He put his arm around her as he folded up his plans. "Don't worry, *mi amor*. I have good reasons for doing this."

They moored in the same cove as before. The sight of the striated cliffs, the sapphire water as it slapped against the pristine sand, tugged at Jane's heart, and she had to look away. Everything reminded her of the first time they had made love. She saw the rock she had been sitting on when he rose from the sea like a god. She saw the stretch of beach where they had given themselves to each other.

Only she had given Francisco more than she had taken from him. He gave his body. She gave her love.

But he did care for her. She knew that. When they were together, it was as if no one else existed—not Hortensia, nor Esperanza, nor any of the others. He was completely with her, his attention focused on her alone. He wasn't thinking about football or washing his car. He wasn't even thinking about another woman. Every thought, every action, spoke of his total absorption with her. No American man had ever been so attentive. Was that why Spanish women loved their men in spite of their infidelity? Was that what Celia was trying to tell her?

She came away from the railing and watched Francisco directing the lowering of the dinghy. He wore jeans, hugging his hips and thighs and tapering to his ankles. His leather belt was stamped with a shell design, the brass buckle a scene of sea gulls above sloping hills. It flashed in the sun as he leaned forward, helping Ernesto load the toolbox into the rowboat. He wore no shirt, exposing his lean, cinnamon back to the golden Mediterranean sun.

Glancing down at her cutoffs and T-shirt, she wondered what his other women wore when they were on his boat. Did they braid their black hair into ropes that trailed down their backs? Or were they always fashionably coiffed? Did he prefer women who never left the house without artfully concealing their flaws first? He had seen all of hers. Or nearly all. He had no idea she had committed the fault of falling in love with him.

His other women. She smoothed her shorts. If she had any self-respect, she'd keep her distance. She should tell him she didn't want to sleep with him anymore.

But she wouldn't tell him that. She'd never been able to stay away from him, and their final parting would come soon enough.

He ambled over to her and put his arms around her neck, pressing her back against his chest. "Well, *jefe*, your men are awaiting your orders."

"Francisco, this is absurd!"

"Ah, where is my independent lady? I thought you were qualified to go treasure hunting!"

She whirled around. "Don't make fun of me!" she cried, her voice breaking. "Not now!" She hit his chest with both her fists.

He caught them easily. "Jane, what's wrong?" he asked, honestly surprised. "I was only joking with you."

"I'm not in a joking mood. Leave me alone."

But he wouldn't. He brought her juice, massaged her back, and finally persuaded her into the dinghy for the short row to the cove. The men grouped around her in a semicircle while she told them what to do. Francisco acted as translator, and nothing more, preferring to stand by and let her give the orders.

They set to work at once, leaping to fulfill every instruction she gave them. She couldn't detect any hostility or resentment—nothing except the same confusion she felt herself. The camaraderie they had shared the night before was gone.

She wondered if it had been genuine in the first place. Francisco claimed all along that their overtures were insulting to her. Had he been right? She reflected that they had never joked and drunk with Francisco either. Perhaps this was a sign of respect in Spain. She didn't know.

But she was grateful, in a way, that Francisco had forced this job on her. If he hadn't, she might have hidden in her cabin for the rest of the hunt, just to avoid the men. This way, they had to work with each other again. And they had to deal with her as a superior, not an equal! It was probably a totally new experience for them.

As the day wore on, she realized that her role as supervisor was more symbolic than anything else. Carlos and Hans knew perfectly well how to build a mailbox without her orders, but they waited for her to tell them the steps anyway. She finally saw that was how Francisco had wanted it, although she didn't understand why. To punish the men, he had said. But also to teach them . . . what?

It took hours to build, but Francisco proclaimed it a job well done. The men were quiet when he praised them and Jane. But they brightened when he told them that they wouldn't camp on the beach, but use the twilight to begin their journey back to the wreck.

"I'm going to lie down for a while," Jane told Francisco. "I'm exhausted."

"You have a right to be," he said. "I'm very proud of you, Doña Juana."

"Thanks," she said feelingly, her eyes lingering on the pleasing curve of his lips.

She hoped he would follow her to her cabin. But he stood on deck, hands on his hips, watching her as she disappeared belowdecks.

She tossed in her sleep, dreaming of pirates and treasure and mermaids. And Francisco, her corsair. Always Francisco. . . .

*   *   *

It was late when she went back on deck. From the galley she smelled the heavenly fragrance of onions cooking in butter. Her stomach rumbled. In the excitement of the day, she hadn't eaten much.

"Hey, Ricardo," she called, hurrying to the galley. "That smells so wonderful! I—"

Francisco stood at the stove, an apron tied around his waist. There was a spatula in his hands, and tears were running down his cheeks.

"What's wrong?" she cried. "Did you hurt yourself?"

He looked sheepish as he wiped his eyes on the hem of his apron. "No."

"Francisco, please, can I help?"

"No."

"But—"

"It's the onions, *querida*. They make me cry."

She laughed, amazed that she could still do it. She hadn't had much cause lately. He gave his shoulders a dignified shrug and turned back to the stove.

"This is the twentieth century," she drawled, coming toward him. "Men are allowed to cry, too."

"Not over onions, *maja*." He grinned at her. "Did you really think I was crying? I mean, truly crying?"

She nodded. "You looked rather stricken."

"So I was. But tell me this: how does a nice American hamburger sound?" He pointed to two patties of raw ground beef sitting on a plate.

She didn't have the heart to tell him that she didn't much care for hamburgers. That had been Uncle Chuck's specialty when she was a little girl. Every now and then, he would decide that he should cook dinner for her. The menu was always the same: hamburgers, potato chips, and frozen green beans. It was Chuck's idea of a balanced diet.

Masking her lack of enthusiasm with a weak smile, she poked one of the patties tentatively.

"Jane, I haven't cooked them yet," he admonished. "I know how to cook hamburgers."

"Oh?"

"*Sí*. My family loves American food." He stirred the onions with a deft motion and gave the pan a shake. "Pizza, egg foo yong—"

"Very American," she observed.

"—hot dogs, and sauerkraut!" he finished proudly. "Do you know how difficult it is to get American hot dogs in Spain?"

"But you always get what you want," she said, feeling a rush of pain.

He gave the onions another stir. "No. No man is that blessed."

She opened a cabinet and pulled out two glasses. They clanged together discordantly. "Is there some wine?"

"But of course. Tonight we have something special. Something to celebrate with!"

"And what is the occasion we're celebrating?"

"Our switching of sex roles, *naturalmente*. You build the mailbox and I do the cooking."

"Oh." What were you expecting? she chided herself. That he was celebrating your discovery that you're sharing him with half the women in Spain?

"It's good wine," he went on, wiping his hands on his apron and grabbing the corkscrew. "*Vino de país*. It's brewed privately by a friend of Emilio's."

Jane handed it to him.

Blowing her a kiss, he uncorked the bottle, then poured out the rich red liquid. He raised his in salute, handing Jane the other one. "Health, money, and love," he said. "And time to enjoy them."

They clinked glasses. The wine was rich and astringent. Francisco closed his eyes, savoring his first taste.

"Good, eh?" He set it down and went back to his cooking.

Whistling a tuneless song, he snitched some onions while he dumped them onto a plate. Then he put the patties in the pan.

There was an air of domesticity about him that made her feel even sadder. She could see them together, in their own kitchen, cooking side by side on a balmy Spanish night. With perhaps a child tucked in bed, dreaming of pirate ships and sunken treasure, like his papa. . . .

The galley was becoming hot, the air greasy. Perspiration beaded on Jane's forehead. "I . . . I need to go on deck," she said.

He frowned. "Are you ill?"

"No. I'm all right."

His hand brushed her hip. "Jane, stay with me," he said. There was an odd catch in his voice. Wrapping his hand around her finger, he studied her short nail, stroking it with the tip of his thumb.

"The hamburgers are burning," she breathed.

"No. They're fine. Don't run this time." Lifting his glass, he pressed it against her damp forehead. The glass was cool.

"All right." She took the glass from him and sipped from it.

"Hamburgers and onions," she said, breaking the mood. "What else are we having?"

"I wanted to have corn on the cob, but you know we Europeans don't eat it. And Ricardo never buys it. Corn is for pigs—and Americans." He chuckled. "Me, I love it. Your uncle taught Alejandro how to cook it. We had some at the fiesta where we became partners." A cloud crossed over his features. "Ah, well, enough of him," he muttered.

He went on with his cooking. His intensity was endearing as he bustled around the galley. He was almost childlike in his concentration.

"So we're having zucchini and tomatoes instead. I hope you like them. Its a recipe Ricardo taught me when we were doing a salvage job near Greece." He lifted the lid of a steel pot.

"Everything's ready. I thought we'd eat at the bow. The moon is fantastic tonight, and it'll be very pleasant."

He arranged everything on two plates, asking Jane to bring the silverware and the wine.

Hans passed them as they made their way through the starlight. "*Buenas noches, jefe*. Doña Jane." He gave her a tentative, apologetic smile. Startled, she smiled back. Then he walked on.

"You see? They're already showing you more respect. As I am," he added. "Look out for that rope. Don't trip, *mi amor*."

The stars were a thousand silver dots in a licorice sky, the moon a tangy slice of lemon candy. Francisco had laid two towels on the deck. They sat on them, cross-legged, arranging their plates in their laps and positioning the wine between them. Then Jane tried her hamburger patty. Her brows lifted. It was unlike any other she had ever had, spicy and delicious.

"My secret recipe," he explained, enjoying her reaction. "Do you like it?"

"It's really meat, isn't it? I mean, it's not eel or something?"

His smile was nostalgic. "I was proud of you that night, when you ate the eel. Ricardo worked so hard to please you."

"I know how it feels to knock yourself out for somebody," she answered.

They finished eating. Then Francisco reached behind a stack of crates and brought out his guitar. Tuning it, he began to hum a plaintive melody. His eyes fastened on her as he sang, moving his fingers across the strings. The guitar echoed his tune in a haunting counterpoint.

His voice was resonant and deep. Though she didn't understand the words, she understood the emotion of his song. He sang of sorrow and regret, of loss and loneliness. He sang everything that was in her heart.

Soon I'll leave, she thought, leaning her head against the crates. And he'll sing this song to someone else.

A tear slid down her cheek. Francisco played on, concentrating, his sibilant Spanish urging more tears to follow the first. She looked at the water, avoiding him, struggling not to let the music affect her so much.

But it was so moving, so very sad. It touched her to realize that the hardness of his life had left its mark. His short childhood. María. Francisco knew a lot about heartache, as well as pleasure.

The song ended. He rapped against the guitar with his knuckles, then set the instrument down and crossed his arms.

Jane picked up her glass. "That was beautiful," she said. "I've never heard anything like it."

"Emilio wrote it for Celia last year. He had to go to France for three months to help with some radar. She saved all his letters in one of her shoeboxes. And he saved all of hers in another one." He looked at her. "They're very much in love, Jane."

She poured herself another glass of wine and took a large gulp.

Moving the bottle aside, he knelt before her, touching her face. "Your cheeks are wet. Did my song make you cry?" His lips found the tears and kissed them away.

Shakily she set the glass down and shut her lids.

His hands slid under her jaw and eased down her throat. "The nights we have spent, *mi amor*. They're precious to me, as priceless as all the gold aboard *El Corazón*." He caressed her shoulders. "Come to me," he murmured, nuzzling her neck. "Come and give me your treasure." His chest expanding, he pulled off her shirt.

She drew her hands protectively across her breasts.

He pried her fingers away. "No one will see, Jane. No one will disturb us." Before she could protest, he unhooked her bra, letting it slip into her lap. "I want to see the moonlight on your skin," he breathed. "I want to memorize every inch of you." Leaning over, he traced her silhouette with his tongue.

Jane arched involuntarily, succumbing to the fire that leaped inside her. Waves of heat radiated from her loins, coursing through her blood. His hands found her hips and his thumbs pressed on the increasingly sensitive flesh of her abdomen. She caught her breath as he lowered her onto the towels. The moon hung above her, cloaking her in a ring of gauzy light.

He took his wine and drank some, then pressed her lips open with his and let the wine trickle into her mouth. It was warm and heady. Her heart skipped a beat as his tongue found hers. The flames rose in her, higher, stronger, hungrier. Francisco groaned and gathered her up in his arms. He rocked back on his heels and cradled her head against his chest. His heart throbbed against her cheek.

"Were there ever two like us before?" he whispered, rising to his feet. She put her arms around his neck, feeling vulnerable and naked.

He must have sensed her feelings, because he bent down and retrieved her T-shirt and bra, then draped one of the towels over her and carried her into the navigation cabin. The maps and other documents fluttered when he opened the door, settling again when he closed it.

Carefully he set her on the floor. "My treasure," he said, brushing her hair away from her eyes. He began to undress. "You are my treasure, you know," he said. "Mine alone. The captain's share."

He lay beside her. She studied his body, from the dark tan of his chest to the paler skin of his hips, where his swim trunks concealed his masculinity from the kiss of the sun. He was her conquistador, the conqueror of her body, her heart, her will.

She drew in a ragged breath as he rained a shower of kisses over her shoulders and breasts. First he had put her in charge of the mailbox. Then he had made her dinner. And tonight he was more subdued, gentler. Was he changing in other ways as well? Secret ways, that a proud man like him would be loath to admit? Those women . . .

"Tonight, we do what you want, Jane. Whatever you desire, you have but to tell me. I'm your slave." He brushed his silky hair over her chest.

"Francisco, you . . . Why are you doing this?"

He kissed her. "You know, *mi amor*. You know."

They made gentle, sweet love in the navigation room, and it seemed as if all his care was for her pleasure. Then he dressed her as if she were his little child, carefully guiding her hands into the armholes of her T-shirt, lovingly sliding her shorts over her quivering flesh. He carried her into his room and his bed, and holding her, he sang to her, his voice barely a whisper, until she fell asleep in his arms.

She awoke alone, his scent still lingering on the bed. She placed her hand on the mattress. It was still warm. He'd left only moments before.

Sighing, she rolled over, trying to sort out her feelings. The hurt was still there, but there were other things, too. Their relationship was like an onion, complex and many-layered. Each time she peeled away another layer, she cried. But at the center was Francisco, with his words of love and his intense passion, and so the tears had been worth it.

Until this last, when she had discovered that there were other fingers plucking at the layers.

She let her arm dangle over the side of the bunk. It brushed against a piece of folded paper. Jane smiled faintly, taking in the messy room—the sweatshirt and shorts lying in a heap, the pile of maps, the leather sandals.

She picked up the paper and started to put it on his desk. Glancing at it, she saw that it had been labeled "Captain's Share" in English as well as Spanish. He had written it in heavy, bold letters. What did Francisco think of the captain's share?

Feeling a mild twinge of guilt, she unfolded it.

There were two columns of writing, one in Spanish and one in English, as if it were a translation. Her eyes widened as she began to read.

"The mermaid is the captain's share," it said. "She possesses the best of the treasure. A heart of gold, eyes of sapphire. Her mouth is the most perfect ruby. In her hands she carries a gilded rope. An untold fortune of silver. Alejandro has no idea. He thinks himself so clever, but I'll keep her for myself. . . ."

"Jane? Are you awake, *mi amor*?" Francisco rapped on the door. Hastily she refolded the paper and laid it on his desk.

He knew about the captain's share after all! Why had he questioned her about it? To see if Alejandro had heard of it?

"Yes, Francisco, I'm awake," she rasped. Was he planning to cheat Alejandro? Oh, no, not Francisco! He wouldn't!

He opened the door and smiled at her. "Good morning, my love. Did you sleep well?"

"Yes, yes, I did." Another layer? One of dishonesty? Lying?

"Francisco . . ." she said suddenly, raising herself on her elbows.

He came into the room and sat beside her on the bed, kissing the corner of her mouth.

"Yes, *querida*?"

"What . . . what would Celia do if she caught Emilio stealing?"

"What do you mean?" His smile was puzzled. "He'd never do such a thing. Emilio is the most honest man I know."

"Oh."

He leaned forward, peering into her eyes. "He didn't do anything, did he? He didn't make a pass at you!"

"No," she assured him. She was probably being silly.

Maybe Francisco had just been doodling. Daydreaming, the way she did sometimes.

"Then hurry and dress. We're going down one last time before we start using the mailbox!" He patted her thigh through the sheet and rose to leave.

"All right," she said quietly. "I'll be right there."

Chapter Ten

❧

The submerged work site was like a scene from *Twenty Thousand Leagues Under the Sea*. The balloons wafted with the movements of the men as they hacked at the coral and rock. Clouds of sand and dust billowed around them like smoke curling in slow motion.

In their scuba gear, Francisco and Jane hovered above the activity. The largest coral mound had been cut down the middle, forming a small ravine. It was here that they had removed most of the coral. Francisco had explained that the shape of the growth indicated that the vessel had lain on its side while the coral grew over it. No doubt the wood had completely decomposed, but the shape remained, like a fossil.

Carlos was vacuuming the center of the ravine with the air lift, a long tube filled with rushing air, sending the debris to the surface. There it would be dumped on the tarp, along with the loads they had sent up in the wicker basket. Jane itched to join in, but Francisco glided away, gesturing for her to follow.

They swam together through the tinted water. High-voltage tension surrounded Jane as she surveyed the excavation. They were so close to discovering the identity of the wreck. Was it the *Corazón*? What if it proved to be a worthless hulk, and not the prize they sought? The thought was too dismaying to contemplate.

She concentrated instead on the changes in Francisco. Perhaps he did love her after all. Perhaps he had been struggling to prove it. She adjusted her mask, breathing steadily through the regulator. She was uncovering her own trove of mysteries. Would she discover nothing but false hopes and silly daydreams? Or would she strip away the protective barriers of pride and find the greatest treasure of all—Francisco's love?

She didn't know. She might never find out.

Francisco hailed her, pointing to Hans, who was busily loading another pile of rocks and coral into the wicker basket. The man paused and waved at Jane, crossing his fingers. Smiling, though he couldn't see her face, she did the same. At least she had found friendship among these macho Latin men. That was something.

They moved on. Jane scanned the bottom idly. Then she saw something glinting among the strands of kelp a few yards away from the site. She circled it, keeping her eye on the spot. Sure enough, something was there!

Remembering the first time this had happened, she mentally marked the area as best she could, then caught up with Francisco. Tugging on his fin, she finally convinced him that she didn't want to play, but that she'd found something.

Together they returned to the spot. Jane led the way, searching among the abundant kelp like a little girl on an Easter-egg hunt. Francisco did the same.

Then she saw it. It was a gold coin! The first find! The first treasure! For a moment she stayed immobile, staring down at the gleaming disk. A rush of emotion welled up in her. Fatima's hopes and dreams lay in her hand. So did Francisco's.

With shaking fingers she gripped it tightly and carried it back to Francisco. As soon as he saw it, he held it above his head and shook his fists. He caught her up, crushing her against him. They whirled in a circle, delirious with triumph. They had done it! Victory was at hand!

Together they streaked back to the kelp and pawed through it. Francisco raced over to the excavation and showed the coin to the others. From her post Jane watched as they went wild. Bouncing like springs, they embraced each other, leaping through the water as the coin was passed around. Clouds of dust rose, so thick that Jane couldn't even see the men.

Hans hurried back with Francisco. The three of them searched through the green plants, but there was nothing else.

Francisco indicated that he wanted to surface. Jane followed him, eager to see the coin in daylight. She couldn't believe it—that she would be the one to find the first piece!

As soon as she was on deck, Francisco picked her up and kissed her wildly. "It's the right century!" he cried. "It could be *El Corazón!*"

"Oh, Francisco!" She laughed. "It's so wonderful!"

"As are you, *maja!*" He threw back his head. "*Gracias a Dios!* I've got the *Corazón!* Ricardo, champagne, *por favor!*"

Ricardo ran from the galley with two open bottles. He dumped one all over Jane and Francisco, kissing their cheeks, shouting, "*Olé! Olé!*" in a high, excited voice. Francisco kissed him back, his hearty laughter drowning in a gurgle as he guzzled the champagne.

"Time for the mailbox!" he announced. "Tell the men to get up here!"

But they were already surfacing, calling and cheering. Scrambling onto the deck, Hans and Carlos lifted Jane on their shoulders and carried her off.

"Doña Jane!" they shouted. "Doña Jane!"

Champagne bubbled everywhere. The men called her name over and over, pressing around her in a clump as they paraded her around the boat.

"Doña Jane!"

Ernesto grabbed a towel out of the galley and threw it around her shoulders. José Luis crowned her with Ricardo's colander. For a scepter, they gave her a broken spearfishing rod.

"More champagne!" Francisco called, laughing. "For our queen! La Reina Juana!"

"La Reina Juana!" the men chanted. Ramón dropped to his knees before her and babbled in Spanish.

"He wants you to knight him!" Francisco chuckled.

She giggled. "All right!"

Hans and Carlos let her down. Then she tapped Ramón on the shoulder and proclaimed, "I dub thee Sir Ramón, Knight of *El Corazón*!"

They hooted. Ramón rose and flung his arms wide. The others bowed in mock respect.

"Champagne!" Ricardo cried, bringing three more bottles. The corks popped in a three-gun salute.

Francisco held up his hand. "Not too much," he said. "We can't dive drunk."

They all settled down after that. Bernardo and Carlos went to test the mailbox. The others refilled air tanks and tinkered with the compressors.

Jane and Francisco walked arm in arm, savoring the moment. She leaned her head against his chest and smiled.

"I can't wait to go back down!" she cried. "Just think, I might find the next piece, too!"

Francisco stopped walking. She could feel his back stiffen. "I'm sorry, *mi amor*, but I can't let you dive anymore."

She whipped her head up to look at him. "What? Why not?"

"It's dangerous with the mailbox in place. I can't take the chance that you'll be hurt."

For a moment she was too shocked to say anything. He took her hand and sat down on a crate.

"I . . . I found the coin," she stammered, staring at him.

He sighed. "I know. But you've got to understand, Jane. I can't risk an accident."

"It's not dangerous!" she protested. "I should know. I built the damn thing!"

"Don't swear," he said tiredly. "I won't permit it."

"You won't *permit* it?" Her voice began to quaver. "Francisco—"

"No. That's final. I won't discuss it." His features hardened.

So he was excluding her from his victory. He was finally

going to uncover the wreck, and she wouldn't even be permitted to see it!

"It's not fair!"

"*Silencio*, woman!" he shouted. She took a step back as if he had struck her.

"I know why," she said in a rush of anger. "I know what you're hiding!"

"What?"

"The captain's share! You don't want Alejandro to know you found it!"

He stared at her, the color draining from his face. "What did you say?" His tone was low and dangerous.

"I saw the paper," she went on, the heat of anger clouding her judgment. "You were describing the captain's share. It was hidden in the mermaid! And you knew it! The other night, you asked me if Alejandro knew about it. Now you want to make sure he never does!" She quailed at the rush of thoughts that followed. "Is that why you've been so loving? To win me over in case I figured out what you were doing?"

"Jane!" He raised his hand.

"No!" she cried. "All your Spanish girlfriends might put up with your macho treatment, but not me, *señor*!"

"How can you say such things?" he thundered.

"Because they're true!" she said, shaking.

"*Hostia*! I can't believe this! You're questioning my integrity!"

"Yes!"

"That is something no Spaniard will stand for, *señorita*, no matter how archaic that may sound to a modern, liberated woman like you! Go to your cabin!"

"With pleasure!"

He rose. His face was white. Clenching his fists, he pushed past her and slammed them down on the railing.

"By the Virgin, I was wrong about you! I thought you had more feeling, but you're just a spoiled brat, aren't you? You think of nothing but what you want to do!"

"That's not true!"

"Liar! You'd jeopardize my entire expedition just so you can have the satisfaction of proving yourself! I've seen how you strut around the men now! I didn't blame them one bit for saying what they did about you! Women who behave like sluts deserve to be treated like them!"

"Look who's talking! You have the nerve to say that to me after you came right out and told me that you've got a whole . . . harem of women? That you'd cheat on any one of them for the sake of your raging Latin appetite? You're really something else, Mr. Macho Man! I feel sorry for any woman who gets mixed up with you!"

"Yes, I know how sorry you feel!" he shot back. "You feel sorriest of all for yourself! You pout and sulk whenever you don't get your way! I worked hard to please you, but you've got such a heart of ice that even a bonfire couldn't thaw it! Thank God the women of Spain have more passion! I would freeze in your arms!"

"Francisco!" she gasped. Pain coursed through her as she saw that he meant what he was saying.

The muscles in his back tightened as he fought for control. Then he turned around. "I hope you enjoyed your summer affair with me. I enjoyed your body. Lucky for me that *all* American women are easy."

Her lips parted. He couldn't have hurt her more if he'd plunged a knife into her.

Lifting his chin, he walked past her with the dignity of a king.

"Please pass the sangría, Miss Burton."

Francisco sat across from Jane on the deck. The others were chatting and laughing, filled with the miracle of the discovery of the coin. Although four days had passed, the wreck itself still hadn't been uncovered, yet their spirits were high.

Wordlessly she handed him the jug of wine. She was sorry,

so sorry. She longed to apologize, but Francisco's chill gaze silenced her. They had hurt each other terribly. She wished with all her heart that she could tell him that she didn't mean what she had said.

But you did mean it, a voice inside her accused. You suspected him of hoarding the captain's share for himself.

Yet deep down, she knew he wouldn't have done such a thing. It was a temporary, fleeting suspicion—the only weapon she had to hurt him with when she lost her temper. Yes, he was right about her: she was a sulky, spoiled brat, used to getting her way.

But was that so horrible? He was the same. If they hadn't been, they might not have endured their difficult childhoods so well. They were both survivors, and sometimes survivors forgot how to compromise.

She felt his eyes on her. He didn't really think she was an easy American, did he? Her throat ached as she replayed their fight in her mind. The things he had said about her!

"Excuse me," she murmured, getting to her feet. She couldn't stand his coldness, not after the volcanic passion that once erupted between them. Hugging her elbows to her sides, she walked to the galley and went inside.

"Hello, Mickey Mouse," Ricardo greeted her. "How d'you do?"

"Hi, Ricardo," she sighed. "Not so good."

He stopped cleaning the sink and looked at her. "Don Francisco, eh?"

Flushing, she nodded.

He pursed his lips. "Many sorry."

"Oh, it's all right. I suppose it's for the best. After all, I don't want to be one of his . . . *cousins*."

He frowned. "You no cousin. You . . . doña."

"No."

She raked her hand through her hair and tried to smile. But her lower lip quivered and she hid it by covering her mouth.

Ricardo clicked his teeth. Opening the freezer, he rummaged around and found a Mars bar. He unwrapped it and cut it in half with one of his sharp knives. "No more," he said, handing her the bigger piece. He began to gnaw on the other one.

"Thanks." They munched in silence. Then Ricardo picked up his sponge and resumed his sink-cleaning.

Jane silently patted his arm in thanks and opened the galley door. From across the deck, Francisco turned. His gaze was stony, empty of any feeling, a look more cruel than any anger.

She walked on. Francisco leaned against the railing, watching her. Then he turned back around, facing out to sea.

She was grateful for his sense of timing. If he had waited just one more second, he would have seen the tears spill over her cheeks.

"*Ya! El barco*! Don Francisco!"

Jane peered out her porthole, dazzled by the early-morning sun.

Hans and José Luis bobbed in the water, their faces upturned as they called out the news. "Don Francisco! *Jefe*!" they shouted jubilantly.

El Corazón had been found!

Jane arrived on deck just as José Luis landed with a thud, water pooling around him. In his arms he carried a gray lump of lichen-covered rock. Advancing, Jane looked closer. It was a cannonball!

Hans appeared at the railing, waving another gold coin. "Doña Jane!" he shouted, grinning broadly.

Francisco appeared, tugging at the buckle of his jeans. His hair was tousled and there were dark rings under his eyes. Apparently he was sleeping as poorly as she was.

He took the cannonball from José Luis and examined it. Then he looked at the coin.

"*Sí*," he said. That was all. The men both looked surprised and disappointed. Don Francisco certainly didn't seem very thrilled!

It's me, Jane thought. I've ruined his victory. Slumping, she sat on a crate and lowered her gaze.

Francisco hurried away. She assumed that he was going to change into his gear.

Hans and José Luis came over to her. "Doña Jane," Hans said excitedly, holding out the relics.

She took them from him, nearly dropping the heavy cannonball. The men laughed. Hans retrieved it while she studied the ball, then rolled it into both of her hands as she braced herself for its weight.

"Wow," she breathed. "These things are over four centuries old!"

Hans cocked his head, chuckling. "Wow," he echoed.

"I wish I could go down with you," she went on. "I'd love to see the wreck!"

They didn't understand her words, but the wistful tone was obvious. Coloring, Hans put his arms around her awkwardly and gave her a friendly hug.

"*Jefe es estupido,*" he said. The boss is stupid.

Just then, Francisco, suited up for diving, raced over and tore Hans away from Jane. His fist crashed against the man's jaw and Hans reeled, tumbling to the deck like a marionette.

Jane jumped up. "What's wrong with you?" she demanded.

Francisco ignored her. He shouted at Hans, who glowered at him but said nothing. José Luis tried to chime in, but when Francisco whirled on him, he clamped his mouth shut.

Then Francisco put on his mask and his regulator, climbed over the side, and splashed into the water.

Massaging his jaw, Hans got to his feet.

Jane rushed over to him. "Are you all right? God, he just came over and hit you! It's swelling! Let me get you a cold rag or something."

His eyes crinkled as he waved at her to stop. "*Por favor,* Doña Jane. I no English."

He put the cannonball and the gold coin on the tarp. Then he gestured to José Luis to follow him back into the water.

He doesn't mind, Jane thought. Francisco can beat him, and he doesn't even blink!

The two men followed Francisco into the water.

Ricardo came up beside her. "Did you see that?" Jane asked, incredulous.

Ricardo shrugged.

"You, Don Francisco *doña*. No Hans cousin." Don Francisco . . ." He slammed his fist into his hand. "Hans understand. He no do."

"Barbarians," Jane breathed, flushing. Was Francisco jealous? Then he had to still care!

But she knew plenty of men who were jealous of women they no longer loved. She'd taught scores of divorced guys who agonized over the romances of their ex-wives. Yet in the same breath they claimed to hate them. Jealousy was not necessarily proof of love. It could have a lot to do with male ego and possessiveness.

"Oh, it's over," she told Ricardo, though she knew he couldn't understand. But she did understand, and she was the one who had to.

Within days, the deck of the *Fortuna* was covered with treasure. Fatima's ransom of golden tiaras, silver scabbards, and emerald bracelets cleaned of their centuries-old encrustations of barnacles, sparkled in the sun. Ricardo told Jane that they had found much more than the corsair had listed in his manifest. The bounty of *El Corazón* seemed endless, as they brought up basket after basket of ruby rings and piles of perfectly preserved diamonds.

There were relics of the ship, too. Two heavy cannon had been lugged over the side and were now soaking in small vats of salt water until Francisco could begin restoration. There was no trace of the ship herself—the sea had taken her long ago. There was also no mention of the captain's share.

Jane wandered down the long rows of magnificent riches, wishing she felt happier about the haul. But her treasure, the love she bore for Francisco, was lost, buried beneath the weight of pain and anger. Sadly she picked up a small gold ring and slipped it on her wedding finger. It fit perfectly.

The jubilant crew brought up more and more each day. Then their finds began to taper off. One day they found nothing. The next was the same. They had found all the treasure.

One morning Jane came on deck to find a powerboat bobbing beside the *Fortuna* and a thin blond man sitting behind the wheel. The crewmen were talking to him with proud swaggers in their voices, bragging and boasting about their exploits on the hunt. Jane smiled faintly as she watched them.

Then Francisco appeared, impeccably dressed in a gray three-piece suit that hugged his hips like the black silk trousers of a Spanish Gypsy. Her throat tightened as she watched him walk across the deck, as graceful as a dancer. The breeze ruffled his wavy hair as he shook hands with the blond man and prepared to board the boat.

He turned. "Miss Burton," he said, indicating that she should come over. Beside him, she felt raggedy in her cutoffs and Mickey Mouse T-shirt. It was almost as if they had all been acting in a play, and Francisco's role was finished. Now he was going back to the real world, the one that existed outside crimson skies and cobalt seas. The world where he had Spanish mistresses, and no time for the American woman who had once loved him. . . .

"You have seen the treasure. All of it," he added harshly. "I've had it cataloged and locked away. Are you satisfied that everything's in order?"

He was so cold to her. She tried to swallow, but the lump in her throat prevented her. Oh, Francisco, she thought, why did we have to end this way? Why didn't we do it better?

"Yes, it's fine," she managed. "I'm sure Alejandro will be pleased."

"No more nonsense about the captain's share?" His eyes narrowed; she could see fire in them as he remembered how she had questioned his honor. Her skin burned from his gaze.

"No."

"*Bueno.* I'm going to deal with the authorities. I'll meet up with the boat in Mallorca. *Adiós, señorita.*"

Their eyes locked. I can't let him leave this way, she thought miserably. I've got to do something!

He began to climb into the powerboat. Jane reached out, hesitated, then touched his shoulder.

"Francisco," she said softly. "I'm . . . I'm sorry." Unable to say more, she turned away.

For a moment, neither moved. Then she heard the boat start up. It sped away from the *Fortuna*.

"*Adiós,* Don Francisco!" Ricardo called, waving. The whine of the engine lessened, then disappeared altogether.

It was too late for apologies. She knew that now. She really had lost him.

Mallorca. The *Fortuna* arrived two hours early. Jane sat with her duffel bag as a customs official arrived to take official possession of the treasure, sitting down with a glass of sangría while he waited for Francisco to show.

There was no reason for her to stay. Alejandro's share was safe. Her part in the hunt was over. There was nothing left but to say good-bye to the men who had fought her presence so bitterly, then had come to respect her.

They hugged her solemnly, one by one.

"*Adiós,* Doña Jane."

"*Adiós, jefe.*"

Ricardo wept as he embraced her. "S'ya later, Mickey Mouse," he sniffled. "You to do, always, *sí?*"

"*Sí.*"

He handed her a little box tied with red ribbon. "You."

"Oh, thank you!" she cried, the tears coming at last. She managed to open it. Inside lay a beautiful lace mantilla. "Ricardo, it's beautiful!" She put it over her hair. It was like a delicate filigree of spun sugar, like fragile snowflakes cascading over her shoulders.

Ricard wiped his eyes and patted her cheek. Then they held each other. It was so hard to say good-bye!

But it was time. José Luis and Bernardo helped her carry her bag down the gangplank to a waiting taxi. She got in, waving at the men as they stood along the railing. Ricardo was crying like an abandoned child.

She waved until she couldn't see them anymore. Then she gave the driver the name of a hotel near the cathedral.

I'm only staying an extra day to recuperate before I go back to San Diego, she insisted to herself. Exhausted, drained, she paced the balcony of her hotel room, scanning the harbor for the *Fortuna*. Francisco must be on board by now. What would he think when he found her gone? Would he, too, regret that their relationship had gone sour? Would he remember her fondly someday, as time healed the wounds they had inflicted on each other?

Below her she heard the tinkle of bells. She glanced down. A young girl sat in a gleaming open carriage pulled by white horses. She was dressed from head to toe in white, her hair covered by a mantilla like the one Ricardo had given Jane. Around her, men walked, serenading her. Farther back, there was a carriage with a young man in it, dressed in a white tuxedo.

It was a wedding party. They were winding their way through the streets of Palma toward the cathedral. Lovely girls in pink dresses surrounded the girl, whose smile was so radiant that Jane could see it from her balcony. The groom was laughing with his friends, joking nervously. The horses nickered, the bells on their bridles jingling with the guitar music.

Fresh tears rolled down Jane's face. It was like a cruel joke, witnessing the joy of others when her heart was breaking.

Grabbing Ricardo's gift, she ran out of her room and into the bustling street.

She wandered for hours, lost but not caring. The wide avenues of Palma were burgeoning with laughing tourists, couples meandering arm in arm, teenagers in shorts and sandals who scampered in and out of the crowds. Jane saw her reflection in a shop window and gasped. She looked terrible.

Then she recognized where she was. Café Hortensia was down the way. If she turned left here, then walked a few blocks more . . .

She came to Francisco's tiny church. Its door was propped open with a brick, beckoning her to come to its sanctuary and rest her poor heart.

Hesitantly she climbed the steps and went in. It was cool and quiet, a comforting haven after the noisy streets. Slipping into the last pew, she bent her head to hide her tears and pressed her fists against her trembling mouth.

"Francisco," she whispered desperately. "Francisco!"

The shadows grew long inside the ancient place. A priest genuflected at the altar, then disappeared through a side door. Still Jane cried, and, in her own way, prayed. She leaned her head against the rail, silent sobs racking her body.

"Francisco . . . Francisco."

Why hadn't she accepted him as he was? Why had she pushed him away? Why did her loss have to hurt so terribly?

Two strong hands raised her lowered head. Soft lips planted a kiss on her brow. Solemnly Francisco slipped the gold ring of *El Corazón* on her finger and pressed her hand against his heart.

"*Por Dios,*" he murmured, his voice quavering with emotion. "I almost lost you!"

Jane's lips parted. Pulling her to her feet, Francisco drew her outside. In the hush of twilight, on the steps of the old church, he crushed her to him and kissed her with all the urgency of a man who has seen the bitterness of life without his soul.

"My foolish male pride," he murmured. "Jane, how can I tell you how I regret the way I've treated you?"

"I . . . I knew about María," she said. "I knew you had a good reason for keeping me out. But I'm not used to—"

"It wasn't María. It was me," he cut in. His voice was tinged with sorrow. "I couldn't admit how much I loved you and respected you. Not even to myself. After all, you would never be like Celia—the obedient little wife I thought I wanted!"

"You . . . *thought* . . . you wanted?" she breathed, meeting his gaze. Her heart leaped with hope.

Grinning ruefully, he shook his head. "My life was so simple before I met you! All I had to do was snap my fingers, and a woman would do whatever I said." He sighed. "Those days are gone forever, I fear."

"Are you sure?" Her hands tightened around his shoulders. The gold ring sparkled in the last rays of the Mallorcan sun.

He frowned, and her heart turned over. "Sure? Do you have any doubts that we must be together, forever? You *will* marry me. Will you marry me? Ah, *mi rosita*, say yes!" He looked so desperate she would have laughed if she hadn't been so close to crying with joy.

"Yes, yes, of course, yes!" she cried, pressing herself against him joyfully, and his answering kiss was all the assurance she needed.

"When I found you gone, I thought I had lost you," he said at last, when they took time for a breath.

"And I thought I had lost you. Especially when you left with that man without accepting my apology."

"I needed time to think," he admitted. "I knew I would have to agree to some changes in order to keep you. There will be no other women, Juanita. Ever. I swear it. And as for

your diving and your career . . ." He winced. "Just make
sure you have enough time for me. And our sons."

"And daughters, *Francis*." Throwing back her head, she
laughed, the sound filled with relief and triumph . . . and love
for this proud man. "I can see I'm in for some changing,
too," she said. "But you're worth it."

"As are you, *mi amor*. You're the treasure I found out on
the sea. That paper you found? It was a love poem."

"The captain's share?" she asked, reddening.

Unconsciously he drew himself up. "*Sí*. You were the
mermaid with the heart of gold. The eyes of sapphire . . ."
He trailed off. "And I would gladly toss everything back to
the ruins of *El Corazón* to prove it."

But Jane needed no further proof. His gaze of love, the
throbbing of his heart against hers, told her all she needed to
know.

"Come, let's get back to the *Fortuna*," he said huskily.
"Ricardo is beside himself." He kissed her again. "Come
my wife."

"Yes, my husband." She slipped her small hand into his.
"Yes."

RAPTURE ROMANCE

Provocative and sensual, passionate and tender— the magic and mystery of love in all its many guises

(0451)

- #1 ☐ LOVE SO FEARFUL by Nina Coombs. (120035—$1.95)*
- #2 ☐ RIVER OF LOVE by Lisa McConnell. (120043—$1.95)*
- #3 ☐ LOVER'S LAIR by Jeanette Ernest. (120051—$1.95)*
- #4 ☐ WELCOME INTRUDER by Charlotte Wisely.
  (120078—$1.95)*
- #5 ☐ PASSION'S DOMAIN by Nina Coombs. (120647—$1.95)*
- #6 ☐ CHESAPEAKE AUTUMN by Stephanie Richards.
  (120655—$1.95)*
- #7 ☐ TENDER RHAPSODY by Jennifer Dale. (122321—$1.95)*
- #8 ☐ SUMMER STORM by Joan Wolf. (122348—$1.95)*
- #9 ☐ CRYSTAL DREAMS by Diana Morgan. (121287—$1.95)*
- #10 ☐ THE WINE-DARK SEA by Ellie Winslow. (121295—$1.95)*
- #11 ☐ FLOWER OF DESIRE by Francine Shore.
  (122658—$1.95)*
- #12 ☐ DEAR DOUBTER by Jeanette Ernest. (122666—$1.95)*
  *Prices slightly higher in Canada

Buy them at your local bookstore or use this convenient coupon for ordering.

THE NEW AMERICAN LIBRARY, INC.,
P.O. Box 999, Bergenfield, New Jersey 07621

Please send me the books I have checked above. I am enclosing $_____
(please add $1.00 to this order to cover postage and handling). Send check or money order—no cash or C.O.D.'s. Prices and numbers are subject to change without notice.

Name_____

Address_____

City _____ State _____ Zip Code _____
Allow 4-6 weeks for delivery.
This offer is subject to withdrawal without notice.

RAPTURE ROMANCE

*Provocative and sensual,
passionate and tender—
the magic and mystery of love
in all its many guises*

(0451

#13 ☐ **SWEET PASSION'S SONG by Deborah Benét.**
(122968—$1.95)

#14 ☐ **LOVE HAS NO PRIDE by Charlotte Wisely.**
(122976—$1.95)

#15 ☐ **TREASURE OF LOVE by Laurel Chandler.**
(123794—$1.95)

#16 ☐ **GOSSAMER MAGIC by Lisa St. John.** (123808—$1.95)

#17 ☐ **REMEMBER MY LOVE by Jennifer Dale.**
(123816—$1.95)

#18 ☐ **SILKEN WEBS by Leslie Morgan.** (123824—$1.95)

*Prices slightly higher in Canada

Buy them at your local bookstore or use this convenient coupon for ordering.

THE NEW AMERICAN LIBRARY, INC.,
P.O. Box 999, Bergenfield, New Jersey 07621

Please send me the books I have checked above. I am enclosing $_____
(please add $1.00 to this order to cover postage and handling). Send check
or money order—no cash or C.O.D.'s. Prices and numbers are subject to change
without notice.

Name_____

Address_____

City _____ State _____ Zip Code _____
Allow 4-6 weeks for delivery.
This offer is subject to withdrawal without notice.

RAPTURE ROMANCE

Provocative and sensual, passionate and tender— the magic and mystery of love in all its many guises

Coming next month

CHANGE OF HEART by Joan Wolf. Man of the world Gil Archer wanted the warmth and love that only Cecelia Vargas, his daughter's riding instructor could give. She married him for love—he taught her passion. But Gil still had to learn that love wasn't meant to be taken and ignored. Would that lesson cost him Cecelia?

EMERALD DREAMS by Diana Morgan. Suzanne Lawrence vowed she'd never again be seduced by dazzling poet/playwright Jay Monahan. No longer the innocent coed overwhelmed by his genius, she was a woman in charge of her life as a professor and critic. But one meeting made Jay her teacher again, guiding her to ecstasy, yet leaving her hungering for the truth behind his love. . .

MOONSLIDE by Estelle Edwards. Knowing she couldn't follow aristocrat Karl Hauptmann back to Germany didn't cool Melissa Merrill's desire. They only had one night, but swore they'd remember it always. Then an unexpected inheritance brought her to him. Did his intoxicating kisses hide a secret ugly enough to destroy their love?

THE GOLDEN MAIDEN by Francine Shore. Suddenly widowed, Maris Verney promised to carry on her husband's latest scientific research. Turning to marine biologist Owen Wyatt for help, she couldn't understand his stubborn opposition to her work, nor could she abandon her suspicions when his taunts turned to teasing, his coolness to caresses. How long could she resist the desire threatening her very heart and soul?

TELL US YOUR OPINIONS AND RECEIVE A FREE COPY OF THE RAPTURE NEWSLETTER.

Thank you for filling out our questionnaire. Your response to the following questions will help us to bring you more and better books. In appreciation of your help we will send you a free copy of the Rapture Newsletter.

1. Book Title:_____

   Book #:_____ (5–7)

2. Using the scale below how would you rate this book on the following features? Please write in one rating from 0–10 for each feature in the spaces provided. Ignore bracketed numbers.

(Poor) 0 1 2 3 4 5 6 7 8 9 10 (Excellent)
                                        0–10 Rating

Overall Opinion of Book............... _____ (8)
Plot/Story............................ _____ (9)
Setting/Location...................... _____ (10)
Writing Style......................... _____ (11)
Dialogue.............................. _____ (12)
Love Scenes........................... _____ (13)
Character Development:
Heroine:.............................. _____ (14)
Hero:................................. _____ (15)
Romantic Scene on Front Cover......... _____ (16)
Back Cover Story Outline.............. _____ (17)
First Page Excerpts................... _____ (18)

3. What is your: Education: Age:_____(20–22)

   High School   ( )1   4 Yrs. College ( )3
   2 Yrs. College ( )2   Post Grad   ( )4 (23)

4. Print Name:_____

   Address:_____

   City:_____State:_____Zip:_____

   Phone # (   )_____(25)

Thank you for your time and effort. Please send to New American Library, Rapture Romance Research Department, 1633 Broadway, New York, NY 10019.